ANOTHER WAY OF DYING

ANOTHER WAY OF DYING

by
FRANCIS CLIFFORD

HODDER AND STOUGHTON

Printed in Great Britain for Hodder and Stoughton Limited, St. Paul's House, Warwick Lane, London, E.C.4, by Cox and Wyman Limited, London, Fakenham and Reading

For
HARRY
and for
JOE

If circumstances lead me, I will find
Where truth is hid, though it were hid indeed
Within the centre.

William Shakespeare: *Hamlet*

1

FORRESTER had seen them twice before—once at Palermo Airport when they were passing through Customs, and once at his hotel in Taormina a few days later. Taormina was where the tourists went and fell in love with Sicily: there had been no earthquakes here. They were an ordinary enough couple by Mediterranean standards—the girl, at a guess, in her early twenties and the man perhaps around fifty, balding, paunchy. The girl wasn't conventionally attractive, though the long blonde hair and the pale blue trouser-suit provided a striking combination; she also had a marvellous flowing walk which made the man appear to strut beside her on his thick, stumpy legs.

On neither occasion had Forrester seen them at close range —first a passing glance and then a bar's-length view. But now they could hardly have been nearer; side by side, the three of them played roulette in the casino at Messina.

Forrester had been so engrossed with the play that he didn't at first notice them move into the vacated chairs to his right. When they eventually caught his eye he gave the girl an instinctive nod of recognition which she ignored and the man didn't catch. The man was next to Forrester and he was sweating a lot; his scalp glistened through the thin black hair and he kept mopping his forehead. Sitting, he was shorter than the girl, but broad, built like a fairground tumbler, with squat, powerful hands. His cheeks were sand-blasted, Forrester saw.

And he staked high—a hundred thousand or two hundred thousand *lire* a time.

The girl now wore an emerald-green dress. Brown, bare arms, a simple gold pendant filling the depression between firm breasts. There was no wedding ring. She placed her own bets, drawing from the pile of chips in front of the man. She wasn't risking too much—a tenth of what he was staking, at the very most. But she won occasionally, and when she did she kept the proceeds apart. The man didn't seem to object: he was losing, losing consistently, and was oblivious of side issues.

"Twenty seven. Red," the grave-faced Italian croupier called. "*Vingt-sept. Rouge.*"

A moment's silence broken by the chips being raked across the green baize—the man's hundred thousand, the girl's five thousand, Forrester's ten thousand, and the rest. Forrester was down about fifty-five thousand, luck running against him now after putting him quickly in credit. But at least he was playing methodically, persisting with the 19–24 bracket, and he wasn't really caring, enjoying the hubbub from half a dozen tables and the recurring tension at his.

He placed his chip as before and the croupier raised an enquiring eyebrow, rake poised.

"*Carré,*" Forrester confirmed, and the chip's position was minutely adjusted. He had one more left, then would call it a night: forty pounds was more than enough to blue.

His neighbour apparently staked at random—first on 7 and then, as the wheel was set spinning, impulsively on 32; a hundred thousand *lire* each. He sat with his hands flat on the baize, not looking at the wheel but waiting, heavy lips pursed, waiting for the ball to rattle home, willing it to lodge where he wanted it. Already he must have lost well over a million—and it mattered, Forrester knew. Tell-tale signs were there.

"*Trois. Rouge. Impair et manque . . .*"

The man grunted and didn't look up. The girl had won a

little on the red. Every so often during the last hour she had touched him encouragingly on the sleeve: this time she sighed audibly, then whispered something, close enough to kiss, and he shook his head.

Again he bet *en plein*, choosing 21. There was no pattern, no discipline, to how he played. It was an expensive way in which to earn sympathy. Forrester's final chip nestled his as the last bets were placed, voices instructing the croupiers and the croupiers repeating the instructions aloud, now in Italian, now in French, now in English. A few onlookers had gathered at their end of the table, as if sensing drama.

"*Rien ne va plus* . . . No more bets . . ."

The ball seemed to take longer than usual to settle.

"*Trente-cinq. Noir.*"

The buzz of comment, the rattle of losing chips against the rake. Forrester started to push back his chair and the act of leaving unexpectedly made the man turn to him.

"You, too—eh?"

It was a coarse face, a kind of desperation showing in the eyes.

"Yes, indeed," Forrester smiled wryly, and moved under the chandeliers to the alcove where the bar was situated.

"Someone in trouble over there?" the bartender said. "The Englishman—the one with the blonde?"

"He's an American," Forrester answered in Italian. "And trouble depends on what you can afford."

The bartender shrugged and sidled away, looking narrow-eyed towards the tables. Waiters came to him with more than orders; he didn't miss much. Forrester sipped a whisky soda. There was quite a crowd standing round where the man and the girl were and he couldn't see them very well. But presently she emerged and walked over to the cashier. Slim legs, and again that smooth relaxed stride. She handed what looked like a cheque to the cashier who studied it, pinged a bell for the

11

manager, conferred with him, then nodded, suddenly obliging, all smiles for a lady.

Forrester drained his glass and made his way to the exit. As he passed the table at which he had played the girl had already returned and was spilling a fistful of chips in front of the man.

You fool, Forrester thought, glancing at him. You bloody fool.

The doorman offered a bored nod as Forrester stepped out under the vast stars. It had just gone midnight. His car was parked beneath the tamarisks, greeny-white in the starlight, and he got in and drove the fifty-odd kilometres back to Taormina, cruising, relaxed, the air like warm silk against his skin and Etna looming on the one hand, the dark smooth sea on the other.

2

A CRY woke him. For a moment as he stirred he couldn't remember where he was or whether the cry belonged to an abandoned dream. Sunshine slanted brilliantly into the hotel bedroom. Beyond the open window and the patterned veranda the horizon was smudged with an obliterating haze.

"Please . . ." he thought he heard.

He pushed himself on to an elbow, head cocked doubtfully.

"Please"—louder this time, seemingly closer, the voice charged with hysteria.

He rolled off the bed and went at once to the veranda. He

had never heard the girl speak and wasn't aware that she was sharing the room next to his, yet his surprise at seeing her was muted, her agitation totally demanding as his wits surfaced.

"What's the matter?" A six-foot gap separated their veranda railings.

"It's him . . ." She had her hands to the sides of her head. "Frank."

"What about him?"

"He is dead."

The back of Forrester's neck prickled. Seconds must have elapsed before his voice came.

"I'll be round," he said. "Let me in."

He grabbed his pyjama top as he kicked into his slippers, then hurried out into the corridor. The first door along was ajar, the girl waiting in the tiny lobby.

"Come. Oh come." She was beside herself.

The man was on his back on one side of the bed. A night's beard-stubble accentuated the awful pallor of his face. Instinctively Forrester searched for a pulse-beat in the wrist, then, failing to find one, slid a hand under the flowered pyjamas and pressed it against the matted chest-hair above the heart, his mind at breakneck speed, thoughts and feelings colliding again and again.

Nothing. Not a tremor. And the fleshy skin felt cold.

"How long ago—?" he began.

"Just now. Five minutes, when I woke . . . Oh God."

He snatched up the phone.

"I want a doctor urgently. There's a man dying here. Yes, here. As fast as you can."

Dying, he'd said, and she fastened on to it. "You mean—?"

"I don't know . . . Have you any brandy?" She was looking at him dazedly. "Have you?"

"No."

He used the phone again, flicking the rest, and asked for

13

some to be sent up immediately, adding: "What about the doctor?"

"I am calling one now."

"It's urgent. For God's sake hurry."

The man looked enormously peaceful, out of reach, not caring. There seemed to have been no knowledge of pain; no fear. An empty glass stood on the bedside table: Forrester picked it up and sniffed, and learned nothing. No bottle, no phial—inevitably he was searching for the obvious things. A travelling-clock showed seven twenty-five.

With an effort he said: "Did he have heart trouble?"

The girl seemed baffled.

"How long have you known him?"

"A few weeks."

"Did he lose much?"

"Lose?"

"Last night. At the casino."

It was cruel at such a time. Even so she might have answered, but there was a knock at the door and Forrester went to open it.

"You asked for cognac, *signore*."

In addition to the bottle the waiter had brought a tray carrying a corkscrew, glasses and a siphon of soda. Habit harnessed him even in an emergency. He seemed eager to come in, to witness something, but Forrester took the tray.

"Is it the *signora*?"

"No." Lowering his voice, Forrester said: "Fetch the manager, will you?"

He shut the door. As soon as he managed to extract the cork he slopped some brandy into a glass and sat on the edge of the bed. He put one hand behind the man's head, lifting, then inserted the glass between the thick lips. Most of the brandy seemed to dribble down the beard-stubble and into the crease-rings in the neck.

Without hope he felt for a pulse again, and again there was

14

nothing. He lowered the man's head back on to the pillows; close-to the pitted cheeks had a bluish tinge. Anything now was too late, hours too late, and the girl must have known it. She gazed at him, hugging herself as if the room were freezing.

The phone buzzed.

"Yes?"

"The doctor is on his way. He will be a few minutes only."

It had all happened too fast for Forrester, so fast that disbelief still had a foothold in his mind; he could hear laughter from the street below and a radio throbbing near by. He eased himself to his feet and poured a brandy for the girl. "Here."

She shook her head.

"Go on. You need it."

She was wearing a short, partially-transparent nightdress. He watched her sip the brandy, screwing her face as she did so.

"Was he like this when you woke? Exactly like this?"

She nodded, swallowing.

"You didn't hear anything during the night?"

"No . . . No."

There was a dressing-gown hanging on the door. "Put this on," Forrester said, going for it. She obeyed woodenly. It must have belonged to the man because the striped towelling enveloped her like a sack, giving her the elongated arms of a clown. But farce had no place here; the body on the bed seemed to fill the room with its presence.

Forrester said gently: "Don't you reckon you'd be better off outside?"

She appeared to have no will of her own. "All right." A slow shudder moved through her. He followed her on to the veranda where she clasped the railings and stared over the tumbling terraces and rooftops to where the sea lay deep as violets among the rocks. Almost inaudibly she asked: "Have you a cigarette?"

15

"In my own room."

"There are some inside."

He went back in and found a pack and lighter on the dressing-table. Under the wash-basin were numerous pieces of metal foil which he hadn't noticed before; he stirred them with a foot, but no more than that; chance had involved him enough as it was. Outside again he lit a cigarette for the girl: her finger trembled violently as she craned close.

"Sit down," he suggested. "Why don't you sit down? We can only wait."

He could think of nothing else to say. The questions chasing through his mind were best not asked. All he could do was silently to urge either the doctor or the manager to come; until then nothing would seem quite real. Along the street a couple of men talked in an angle of shadow and a gull planed low overhead, blinking the sun. Another morning, another day. It was incredible. A quarter of an hour ago he'd been asleep.

"Frank," the girl sobbed quietly now. "Oh God . . . Frank."

The doctor was the first to arrive. He was small, bustling and abrupt: other people's tragedies were routine.

"This man is dead," he announced, straightening up, and somehow he contrived to make it a complaint.

"I know," Forrester said. The girl had remained on the veranda.

"I was told otherwise."

"I hoped otherwise—to begin with."

"He's been dead for hours."

"If you say so."

The doctor picked up the bottle of brandy. Disapprovingly, he said: "You gave him this?"

"I tried to, but I don't think much went down . . ." A second knock. "*Scusi.*"

Now it was the manager—hastily dressed and with eyes not

16

yet fully alert. He was tall for a Sicilian. Forrester let him in and he pushed anxiously past into the bedroom: it seemed to surprise him to find the doctor there and he stopped short like someone at sword-point.

Staring at the body he said: "How is he?"

"He's finished."

"*Finished?* . . . But—"

"Finished," the doctor repeated.

"No!" The manager crossed himself with a kind of reflex movement. "Why? What happened to him?"

A quick shrug. "All I know is what you see."

The doctor went to the basin and ran the taps.

"Who found him like this?" the manager wanted to know. "Who—?"

Forrester said: "The young lady did." He nodded towards the veranda: it was blurred by the mosquito-frame on the windows. "She's out there. She called me round when she realised what had happened."

"When was this?"

"About twenty minutes ago. I rang for the doctor and then asked for you to be informed."

The manager eyed Forrester's pyjamas. He was either slow-witted at such an hour or on the brink of some crude suspicion; men in his position must live with them. "And you came as you are?"

"Certainly."

"The woman telephoned?"

"She called from the veranda."

"Was he dead when you arrived?"

"You'd better ask the expert."

Fumbling for a towel, the doctor had discovered the fragments of metal foil beneath the basin. He gathered some of them up and squinted at them closely. The manager moved nearer the bed, hands fluttering.

"How long has the man been dead, *dottore*?"

"Perhaps four or five hours."

"And you can't tell why?"

"Not at the moment." The doctor held a ragged square of foil against the light. "But if you want a guess I would say that he was tired of life."

"He killed himself?"

Another jerky shrug.

"God in Heaven," the manager muttered. "Have you spoken to the woman?"

"I assumed she was his wife, but the answer is no."

The manager started towards the veranda, but Forrester checked him. "It's no use asking her."

"Why not?"

"Give her time. She deserves a little time."

"She will know more than any of us."

"Not necessarily." Forrester gestured at the body. "She was asleep."

"How do you know?"

"She told me." Forrester was slightly nettled. "Look," he said evenly, "let's leave the interrogation to the police, shall we?"

"Of course, *signore*. Forgive me. It is just that . . . well, a suicide is not good for a hotel."

"Adultery but not suicide," the doctor remarked dryly. He lifted the receiver and asked the operator to send at once for the police.

"A priest, too, perhaps," the manager suggested, hands still on the go.

"How can we tell?" the doctor said, hanging up with professional impatience. You must be aware, his sharp dark glance implied, that foreigners have as many creeds and denominations as their luggage has labels.

"The woman might help us."

18

Again the manager started towards the veranda and again Forrester touched him on the arm, if only to spare her a haltingly comic brand of English. "I'll do it."

She was slumped in one of the cane chairs; her face was expressionless. He said quietly: "About Frank—d'you happen to know if he was a Catholic?"

"Please?"

"A Catholic?"

Her lips seemed very dry. She moistened them and Forrester waited, leaning over. He thought she would never answer. But at last she said: "What does it matter?"

"They think perhaps a priest ought—"

"What does it matter?" she said slowly again. "He's dead isn't he?" Then: "I don't know what he was. I . . . I hardly know who he was, even. We never spoke about that kind of thing."

Only now, as Forrester's mind steadied, was it dawning on him that the curiously brittle accent and unusual rhythm of her speech were not somehow the result of shock. But it was no time to wonder about nationalities. Her eyes were absolutely leaden in the fresh light and she looked pathetic.

He said: "Don't you think it would be better if you dressed? You haven't a bathroom here, have you?"

"Bathroom? No."

"You can use mine."

She didn't reply.

"The police are coming, d'you see? They must. It's inevitable, and it's just as inevitable they'll want to ask questions . . . Don't you think getting dressed might be a good idea?"

She rose without saying a word. Forrester made a point of leading the way. The doctor had pulled the sheet up over the body, he noticed.

"We're going next door," he told the manager. Not knowing

19

the girl's name was a handicap, making him sound almost callous. "She wants to get into some clothes before the police arrive—and so do I."

He watched her collect the blue trouser-suit from the closet; handbag and underwear from a chair. It seemed to frighten her to be inside again, inside and close. Not once did she look in the direction of the bed.

In a low voice the manager murmured to Forrester: "About a priest—?"

"She can't say."

A pair of shoes were by the writing-table. "Ready?" Forrester asked the girl and let her go first. Three or four maids and waiters were gossiping in the corridor; they stared, suddenly silent as the two of them turned into Forrester's end room. He showed the girl into his bathroom then kicked his slippers off and got into sweat shirt and trousers. The doctor and manager were on the adjacent veranda now; he could hear the buzz of their conversation. So he went out himself and spoke to them across the gap.

"She ought to stay here—wouldn't you agree? For a while, anyhow."

"The police will expect to see her." This was the manager, still agitated, still ready with suspicions, stroking his blue jowl.

"What's wrong with here?"

Someone was craning over an upper balcony, peering down. The news was spreading, going the rounds with the morning calls. Irritably, Forrester wheeled about and went inside, picked up the telephone and ordered coffee for two.

"Two, *signore*?"

"Yes, two."

Only just gone eight o'clock. Already the day seemed everlasting.

The girl was perhaps five minutes in the bathroom. She had

20

combed her hair but wore no make-up and her face remained blanched beneath the tan.

"I've asked for some coffee."

"Thank you."

"There's no need to return to your own room yet awhile."

"You said the police would—"

"They can speak to you just as well in Number 30 as they can in Number 31."

"You are very kind."

Forrester indicated the veranda and she shot him a nervous glance before stepping out, almost as if she were afraid to face the living too. Seeing them emerge the doctor and manager returned inside, heads together like conspirators. Forrester lit a cigarette for the girl and himself. The sense of unreality still persisted. He'd intended visiting Tindari, but already it was clear he would be doing no such thing. He gazed at the girl again, tongue-tied by the inadequacy of words. She seemed broken; without resources. And he knew that feeling.

"I'm sorry," he said at last. "Very sorry."

"It was so awful . . . awful . . . to find him like that."

"What time did you leave the casino?" When she frowned he went on: "You'll hardly remember, but I was at the same table. Was it late?"

"Sometime after two."

Forrester nodded, blowing smoke. Four to five hours dead— so there had been no hesitation, no agonised lying awake. When the man finally quit the casino and started along the coast-road the decision must already have been made, or was hardening fast. And somehow it had been hidden from her. Yet she must have been blind: Forrester had a vivid picture of the strained, desperate eyes that briefly fastened on to him as he pushed back his chair.

"What was his name?"

"Frank."

"I know," he said quietly.

"Frank Nolan."

"And you're—?"

"Inger."

"Is that Swedish?"

"Norwegian."

"Mine's Neal," he said. "Neal Forrester."

In the narrow street below a police-wagon had appeared, nosing into the hotel's entrance, and Forrester wondered whether she had seen it. A waiter came through to the veranda with the coffee; the room-door must have been left off the catch. The haze had practically lifted from the sea, exposing a ship balanced on the horizon like a small white toy. And soon there were new voices from the room where the man lay dead, crisper, brisk with authority.

The girl crumbled her cigarette nervously in the tray. "What will they want to know?"

"I couldn't say exactly."

"I don't speak Italian."

"Don't worry about that," Forrester said. "I'll help you along." Against his will he was committed. She appeared scared again, in dread of whatever was in store, and pity moved in him. "They'll just want to learn what they can from you, that's all. There's no one else. You were with him, don't you see?"

3

THERE were two policemen, one of whom looked as if he had slept in his uniform; the other one did most of the talking. He was swarthy, with a pencil-line moustache and neat, wiry hair. It was close on half past eight when he led his colleague and the manager into Number 30. The doctor wasn't with them. Cap under arm, the policeman brought his heels roughly together and bowed slightly.

"Would you come in, please?" he said, motioning Forrester and the girl from the veranda. As they entered he enquired needlessly: "Is this your room, *signore*?"

"Yes."

A searching glance at them both. "I have a number of questions."

"Very well."

"They are mainly for the *signorina*. I will speak to you later."

"The *signorina* doesn't know Italian."

"How good is yours?" the policeman asked sceptically. Most tourists came with phrase-books and cameras—click, click, click—went home and forgot.

Forrester shrugged and gave him a sample of slang. "Try me."

"All right, all right." Impressed, his companion started fishing for a notebook. "Now, the lady's name?"

"I'd sit down if I were you," Forrester suggested to the girl. He pulled a chair from under the writing-desk. "They want your full name."

She seemed to come out of a dream. "Inger Lindeman."

Forrester spelt it for the note-taker's benefit.

"Nationality?"

"Norwegian," Forrester replied.

"Address?"

"They also need your address."

She gave it in a flat monotone.

"Oslo?" the man with the notebook queried direct, and she nodded.

"Age?"

"Can't you get most of these things from her passport?" Forrester said defensively, but was ignored.

"Her age?"

"Now they're asking how old you are."

"Twenty-three."

"Married?" the policeman continued briskly as soon as he got the translation.

"No," Forrester said.

"What was her relationship to the deceased?"

Forrester appealed to the manager. "Is this really necessary? And if so, can't it wait? Surely at a time like this—"

"I agree," the manager said, stirring the air in protest. "The relationship is obvious." Then, covering himself. "The register is in order, though. You will see when you make your inspection."

"*Da vero?*" the policeman snapped. "Fancy!" He turned to Forrester. "Ask her what happened last night."

"They came back from the casino at Messina sometime after three, and when she woke up he was dead."

"Ask her, please."

"I already have. She doesn't know anything more."

"I appreciate your intentions, *signore*, but the answers must come from her."

"Okay—but why now? Why not later? She's very shaken. She needs a few hours."

24

With a slight trace of bite in his voice the policeman repeated: "Ask her."

And so it went on—until almost ten o'clock; predictable questions, needless questions, stupid questions. The policeman occasionally presented a pained expression as evidence of sympathy, but the veneer was thin. Not many foreigners died in Taormina, and he was unlikely to have come across one who had died like this; headquarters would expect nothing less than thoroughness.

When did they arrive in Sicily? From where? For business or for pleasure? Did they travel much? What was Nolan's occupation? Had he been unwell? Did he complain at any time of his health? Were the two of them on good terms? Had there been trouble between them recently—yesterday?—last night? Why did they go to Messina? What was wrong with the local casino? Had anything happened last night to make her suspect that Nolan was under more than usual stress? . . . And you, *signore*? Full name? Nationality? Occupation? Date of arrival here? Any connection with the deceased? Where were you this morning when you heard the lady calling? What time was this? . . . And then? And then? . . . It was wearyingly painstaking but, to Forrester's mind, the wood was being missed for the trees. And he finally suggested as much.

"Suicide?" the policeman reacted sharply. "That would be jumping to conclusions."

"The doctor isn't without some evidence."

"He implied that suicide was a possibility—that is all."

'Well, I'm not going to start splitting hairs, but I'd bet you a month's pay he's right."

"You seem very sure."

"I also played roulette in Messina last night." Forrester shot a glance at the girl; she was staring blankly across the room, twitching a cigarette between her fingers. "It made a change to go somewhere else. By sheer chance I was alongside them at the

25

table. When I left Nolan was over a million down and showing every sign of following it with more. He was already right out of his depth—and getting scared."

"That was your impression?"

"Very much so."

"And yet he went on playing."

"You heard what the *signorina* said."

The untidy policeman referred to his notes. "She estimates he lost as much as a million and a half."

"Exactly," the other one commented, pursuing his logic. "And yet she also says there was nothing significant about his manner. No change. No difference. That doesn't sound like a suicide-to-be."

"The watcher often sees more of the game."

"What is that supposed to mean?"

"You've been told that he'd lost on other occasions; it therefore wasn't a new experience for Signorina Lindeman. For my part, though, as an outsider, I reckoned he was in a bad way. Not that I imagined he would kill himself—of course not. People can lose and lose and lose again, yet they go on living. Life is the one thing most of us keep in reserve. But Nolan was certainly in trouble."

Someone rapped on the door and the manager went to open it, listened through the narrow gap then let himself out. Forrester thought he glimpsed a couple of ambulance-men in the corridor.

He continued: "Maybe it wasn't his money in the first place. Who knows? He was a stranger as far as I was concerned. They both were." Once again he glanced at the girl. "And she doesn't know all that much about him herself."

"If you accept that she is telling the truth, *signore*."

"Oh, to hell," Forrester flared. "I suppose the same goes for me as well?"

For the first and only time that morning the policeman

26

permitted himself the ghost of a smile. "Any enquiry has to be determined by the assembly of facts and a comparison of information."

"That sounds as if it's straight out of a training manual."

"It makes sense, *signore*, nevertheless."

"Well, don't waste too much of your time on the girl. She's more in need of help than able to give it."

"She will have to sign a statement. And you also."

"No one's going to object to that."

They started to leave at last, nodding formally, adjusting their caps. "*Arrivederci, signorina . . . Grazie.*" They were pretty human, after all.

"Why," the crumpled one frowned near the door, "should a man deliberately go beyond his depth? One and a half million *lire*—" It was made to sound like unattainable wealth.

"Perhaps he was afraid to draw back," Forrester suggested.

"Afraid?" the other one said. "I don't understand."

"You've seen Nolan. He wasn't exactly a catch, was he? Perhaps failure for him would have meant showing her he hadn't sufficient nerve. God knows. I'm only guessing."

"Then he was a fool."

"He wasn't the first and he won't be the last."

"Maybe so. But it still doesn't follow that he killed himself."

4

I_N the corridor they remembered Nolan's passport. Efficiency wasn't their strong point. Forrester re-entered his own room to ask the girl where it might be.

"She says it's in the drawer of the bedside table," he told them.

The body had been taken away; the clothes were stripped from the mattress. The room seemed strangely empty. The passport wasn't in the drawer, though the girl's was. Nolan's they found in his jacket, which hung motionless in the closet.

The senior policeman flipped them both through. "He was Canadian, *signore*. Born Vancouver . . ." He liked a small triumph. "You said American."

"Well, I said wrong. In any case he was a long way from home." Now it was Forrester who turned to leave. "When do you want us for the statements?"

"At noon? . . . Do you know where the police post is?"

"Oh yes."

"Until noon, then . . . *Grazie*."

They stayed on to search the place, Forrester imagined. When he got back to Number 30 the girl was still sitting in the chair for all the world as if she hadn't moved.

"Thank you for all you have done," she said.

"I'm afraid it isn't over yet. The police want you to go and sign a statement."

"Will you be there?"

"They need one from me as well."

"And then—?"

"There's bound to be a post-mortem, but beyond that I couldn't say."

She seemed to have shed the worst of her distress. Incredibly, almost three hours had passed since her cries had woken him.

"Next door's empty now," he said.

"Empty?"

"Frank's gone. They will have taken him to the hospital."

"Oh." Just that, in a whisper—"Oh."

She got up and went on to the veranda, suddenly restless. Forrester followed her, many things in his mind.

"I'm going to wash and shave. And afterwards—after we've been to the police, that is—tell me what you want to do . . . Okay?"

"Thank you," she said.

They walked when the time came; it wasn't far. Heads turned as they entered the foyer. She was probably used to being looked at because she didn't appear to notice. The manager beckoned Forrester when they were halfway across and he veered over to the desk.

"The *signorina* is being allocated another room—Number 47. Her belongings will be moved there just as soon as the police agree. A smaller room . . . I am sure, if you explain, she will understand."

Forrester nodded. "I'll tell her, anyway." It looked as though he'd become official go-between.

"It is appreciated," the manager said.

The high sun fell on them as they emerged. They turned along the slanting street between walls dripping with bougainvillaea and soon they were hemmed about by the umbrellas of the pavement cafés and the shops stocked with bric-à-brac where the touring coach-parties were let loose. If Forrester had been asked to describe the girl he would have listed blonde, slim, tallish, brown eyes, high cheek-bones. But now, as he

29

moved beside her, he was reminded of Nolan's heavy quick-paced strut, and then he was remembering him at the casino and then thinking of him on the bed only hours ago. Nolan's memory kept pace with them in the noonday glare and amongst the indifferent passers-by, the girl's face set, grief and shock hidden behind dark glasses.

Only once did she say anything. "We were leaving to-morrow. We were going to Rome . . . What will happen about the hotel?"

"They're moving you elsewhere—to another room. The manager told me just now."

"The bill, I mean."

"That's something to think about later." Then, because that seemed insufficient: "How are you placed?"

The phrase defeated her. "Please?"

"How are you for money?"

"Not good," she said. "Not good at all."

It was five or six minutes to the police post—an ochreous, grille-windowed building with the scurf of old election posters disfiguring a side wall. They mounted the shallow steps to-gether to be engulfed by the apparent darkness of the interior. The duty-clerk let them through the barrier without delay and showed them into an office marked *PRIVATO*—largish, white-washed, with a big desk at one end and battered wooden filing-cabinets around two sides. The place reeked of stale cigar smoke. There were three men waiting for them, a grey-faced civilian in a grey suit, the policeman from the hotel who had done the talking and his senior officer—a heavy-jowled, podgy-handed individual with black, button eyes and a smoker's wheeze. Forrester had seen him one day near the Mazzaro beach staring avidly after two retreating, bikini-clad figures, and now he stared without inhibition at the girl for just too long for it to pass unnoticed.

He introduced himself, and when they were seated he said

to Forrester: "I understand you are acting as interpreter for this lady?"

"That is correct."

"We have prepared the statements based on the information you both gave and you will be asked to sign them. This is quite normal procedure. There is nothing unusual or significant about it—is that clear? . . ."

A flip of the fat fingers. The civilian handed some papers across the desk. Perhaps he was a typist, or a lawyer; not that it mattered. The statements were on foolscap, double-spaced, and the girl's filled two pages and a half, Forrester's three-quarters of a page.

"Take your time," the officer wheezed, subsiding into a swivel chair and pretending to examine his finger-nails. No disaster could ever have happened to him.

Forrester turned to the girl and began quietly to translate. A fan squeaked overhead. They had spelt her name incorrectly, after all, but there were no other literals that he could see. *I am Inger Lindeman, Norwegian citizen, of Paul Astrup Vei 26, Oslo, age 23, single, Passport No. 427813, at present in residence at the Hotel Capua, Taormina. . . .* It was a competent précis of what he learned about her from the policeman's questioning. *I met Mr. Francis Nolan six weeks ago in London where I was working in a club, the Golden Cobweb. We went to Paris together, where we stayed two weeks. We were for three weeks after that in Alassio, after which we flew to Palermo, then came to Taormina . . .*

"All right so far?" he asked, and she nodded, eyes closed.

Last night we went to the casino at Messina. We played roulette. I estimate Mr. Nolan lost one and a half million lire. At two-thirty o'clock this morning we took a taxi back to the Hotel Capua, arriving at about three-thirty. We went immediately to bed. I noticed nothing abnormal in Mr. Nolan's manner, either then, or during the journey from Messina, or at the casino . . .

"He was tired," she interpolated. "Frank told me he was very tired."

"No more than that?"

"No."

Forrester let it go.

I awoke at 7.15. At first I thought Mr. Nolan was asleep . . .

There was nothing new, nothing at variance with how she had answered. Forrester's statement was also accurate . . . *Neal J. Forrester, British, of Peterborough, England, age 37. . . .* Both ended with an elaborately worded declaration of their approval and a prepared space for the signature witnesses. The girl signed first, then Forrester: it was soon done.

"Is that all?"

"Yes, *signore*, that is all." The officer glanced cursorily at the documents. "I must compliment you on your Italian."

"Thank you."

"It is exceptionally good. You must know my country well."

"This is my first time in Sicily. But I have relatives in Rome, cousins, and I've visited them for more years than I care to remember."

"Rome?" There might have been a bad taste in his mouth. "Well, no doubt that will account for it." He scrawled his name on the lines provided and the civilian went to work with a rubber stamp. "Now, as regards Mr. Nolan's death. We shall be taking two other statements—the night porter's at the Capua and the manager's; these, it is hoped, will confirm the lady's estimates of times and so on. And your own, *signore*. For the record, you understand?" he added smoothly. "Other routine enquiries will also be made—at the casino, for instance—but naturally our main concern is the autopsy. The earliest we can expect a report is tomorrow afternoon." His button eyes kept straying to the girl, measuring her blatantly. "Perhaps you will

32

be good enough to tell the lady that we shall retain her passport at least until then."

"Are you implying that she's under suspicion in any way?"

"Not at all. Nor, *signore*, are you."

"Isn't that marvellous?" Forrester's astonished sarcasm was lost on the officer.

"But holding the passport is natural in the circumstances."

Forrester shrugged and said to the girl: "We can leave now. They're finished for the time being."

There were thin smiles as they rose, bows, a holding open of doors, nods. "*Grazie, signorina* . . ." But no word of sympathy, no expression of regret, neither then nor at any time. The officer smirked knowingly as Forrester passed: "What would she have done without your help, *signore*? I trust she will realise how indebted she is." Angered, Forrester stepped past him. Instinctively, he gripped the girl's arm. He had no illusions about her, but he could see how vulnerable she was, how hard it must be to be young and attractive and suddenly made alone.

5

THIS was on the Tuesday.

She seemed to dread the thought of going back to the hotel, so he took her down the steep zigzag hill to a fish restaurant near the beach at Giardini. It was quiet there, with few people, and he chose a table on the tiny terrace. She had no appetite, only toying with the food. For the most part they were as distant as strangers, and now and again Forrester found his sense of duty wilting a shade as he thought ruefully of where he might have been—Tindari, or at the swimming-pool, or in chance conversation with somebody; laughing, perhaps. Already it seemed an age since he had laughed. But whenever his mind wandered the girl somehow broke the distraction—this time with a shiver that shook ash from her cigarette.

"Are you cold?"

"No." She narrowed her shoulders, looking away. "Not like that . . . It came from inside." Then: "What made him do it? What could have possessed him?"

Forrester hedged. "What sort of person was he?"

"Always busy, always moving." For a moment a memory trapped her. "Tomorrow was always going to be better, even better. That is why I cannot understand . . . *Cannot*. He was such an optimist."

"It was good with him, then?" Someone had to show an interest; she had a right to it: her kind weren't equipped for loneliness.

"Yes, it was good."

"And yet you hardly knew him."

"True."

"What he did?"

"No."

"Where he was from?"

"He was American."

"His passport says Canadian. It also gives his occupation. He was an agent."

"What does that mean?"

"It could mean many things." A breeze wrinkled the sea, coming smooth and warm, stirring the geraniums planted along the stone balustrade. "When did you go to England?"

"Two years ago."

34

"To work in a club?"

"No—to look after children."

"Are you a nurse?"

She shook her head. "Three children, at Guildford. It was a big house. The name of the people was Osborne, and the children were called Linda and Jonathan and Jeremy."

"And then you left and went to London?"

"I was bored," she said. "First I went to a shop—it was Harrods—and then I heard about the Golden Cobweb. I preferred the hours, and the money was better. I was a hostess there." She drew on the cigarette. "One night, six weeks ago, Frank walked in. And now . . ."

Almost incredulously she ended on an upward inflexion. Now. . . . Everything else was far away, long ago—the black tights and the plunge neckline, Harrods, the *au pair* existence, Oslo. Now was all that mattered, the shock was now, the bewilderment now, the problems here and now.

"Did he speak Italian?"

"Frank?"

"Did he have any languages?"

"No. Oh, no." Her lips formed what might have been the merest hint of a smile. "He just had a way with him—no matter where we were. He was . . . I don't know, things were always possible with Frank around."

Abruptly, as if she regretted the phrase, her eyes blurred again. She was very much like a child, Forrester thought, and with luck the pain and confusion wouldn't last. With luck she'd turn a corner and forget, the way children do. Nolan would diminish, Nolan for whom tomorrow must have been like a post-dated cheque that couldn't be met. She was young and too much would happen to her. Life would soon engulf her again.

He said: "Being practical for a moment—don't be anxious about the hotel bill. You'll only be responsible for the new room."

35

"Are you certain?"

"The management accepted you as husband and wife. I doubt if they'll press you for payment."

"How much longer will I have to be here?"

"A couple of days or so, I suppose."

"I have thirty thousand *lire* only, perhaps a little more."

Twenty pounds, say. "That ought to cover you." At a pinch.

"For the hotel, yes. Maybe . . . But afterwards? How will I manage afterwards?"

"I reckon the best thing will be for you to contact your Consul. There's sure to be one in Palermo. He'll get you home all right."

"Home," she echoed, the eyes blank.

To his surprise, she then said: "Are you married?"

"Why do you ask?"

"You've been so understanding. So helpful."

"Need one be married?"

"Are you?"

"No."

"Were you?"

"Yes."

With luck she would have no scars. A vivid memory was an affliction, bringing anguish in the night.

6

FORRESTER was right about the bill. He spoke to the manager that evening.

"Correct, *signore*. I have no precedent, of course, but as from noon today she will be charged at the rate for the room to which she has been transferred." He quoted the figure. More uncertainly he went on: "And—forgive me—since you seem to have taken her under your wing, if I may say that, perhaps you can tell me what her own financial situation is. I am in a difficult position, as you may appreciate. I am told the police could find no funds, no travellers cheques, belonging to Mr. Nolan, and naturally I am wondering—"

"She can afford the room."

"Ah . . ." Relief showed in the narrow face, followed by a supplementary doubt. "But where will she go from here? Transport costs money, too, *signore*—and, well, she doesn't come from the next town."

Clearly he wanted no further embarrassment. There had been sufficient as it was, more than sufficient. After all, he as good as explained, he ran an hotel, not a charitable institution, and she had been given every consideration in difficult circumstances. "For instance," he had the gall to say, "she will not be billed for the bottle of cognac ordered this morning, although technically—"

"I think you'll find she'll manage," Forrester snapped, amazed.

He was waiting for her in the foyer, one eye on the lift. People were coming and going all the time. It had seemed a mercy to offer to take her somewhere; the hotel's restaurant was no place to be so soon, and outside she needed an escort.

Forrester waited for perhaps ten minutes before she arrived. She was wearing the same short emerald-green dress she'd worn at the casino and, as she came towards him, Forrester reflected briefly that Nolan hadn't exactly dazzled her with the earth—a two-star hotel, a room with no bathroom . . . Had it been the same in Paris and Alassio? Was he scraping the barrel from the first?—or was that squandered million and a half *lire* the last despairing *phut* of a really sparkling firework?

A few feet away a middle-aged couple stopped to observe them, the woman nudging and whispering. They weren't the only ones taking an interest, though they were the most obvious, and Forrester shot them a savage look.

"Hallo," he said to the girl. "Did you manage to sleep?"

"Not really." Strain showed in her brown eyes; they seemed to burn.

"What's the room like?"

"It will do."

The first flash came as they were turning towards the exit. It caught them full face and Forrester blinked. In the same instant he saw a photographer—knees slightly bent, hands coming up again.

"Please," he heard the manager protesting from behind. "No! Not here, please!" Then there was a second flash.

"Come on," Forrester said urgently, and he and the girl made for the door. Palms outward, she was shielding her face.

The photographer skipped backwards in front of them. "One more, *signorina* . . ." He steadied himself, a small man with rimless spectacles and too many teeth, grinning coaxingly. "Just one more—"

"*Basta!*" Forrester pushed him roughly aside. A lens-cap rattled on the floor as the photographer was spun round. "Please!" the manager appealed, nearer now, and to no one in particular. It was all over in a matter of seconds; Forrester and the girl were outside, hurrying down the steps. Neither

38

looked back. In the street they slowed to a walk. Sod him, Forrester fumed. Sod them all . . . The light was patchy in the street, revealing others who also walked, but there were no prying eyes, no bloody whispering. She could cry here and he didn't stop her. In their haste they had come the wrong way and he led her round to the car-park, then headed along the Corso Umberto and followed the coast a few miles south to a restaurant he had previously discovered where they became merely one more couple and no one knew about Nolan, dead or alive. Afterwards, towards eleven, during the leisurely return drive to the Capua, he ran the day through his mind and saw how its pattern had somehow conspired to make him responsible for her.

"Good night, Inger," he said when they parted at the lift on her new floor.

7

THE police officer had suggested that it might be Wednesday afternoon before he was in possession of the findings of the post-mortem. But he had over-estimated either his compatriots' zeal or the local laboratory's capabilities: in any event it was Thursday morning before the result was through.

The whole of Wednesday therefore meant marking time, remaining within easy reach of Taormina. Forrester didn't begrudge it; he had no firm plans and a very full three weeks' leave was behind him, first in Rome, as so often, then here—

here being strictly for winding down after a hectic year. Rome hadn't helped in that direction; it never did. Rome was busy, urgent, endlessly entertaining and demanding. Whereas Taormina was as beautiful a place for idleness as could be. Not that the girl was in any state to appreciate beauty; she was still very much sunk within herself. Forrester found that he was constantly trying to draw her out, not prying but somehow seeking to ease her isolation and the raw ends of yesterday. She could fend for herself before long; but not yet, and certainly not in this place.

Early on there was a reminder for her that she was different from anyone else in Taormina—the newspaper-racks in the shops carried a front-page picture of the two of them. The word "companion" took on a certain significance in print, Forrester thought sardonically, glossing over the caption. He didn't offer her the copy he bought, and she didn't ask to read it. He drove south again, aimlessly, just to get her away and use up the morning. Near Acireale he bought bread and cheese, fruit and wine, and they ate at a vantage point some miles inland, pine-clad hills all around, Etna as a backcloth and the sea glittering like beaten metal in the distance. He taxed her less and less about Nolan and not too much about herself. Mainly he spoke in generalities—doing his best to divert her thoughts from where, inevitably, they sought to swarm. About himself he said almost nothing at all. It was hard going sometimes and there were dragging silences, with occasional attempts at conversation by both of them at the same time.

At one point he said: "I'm leaving on Friday—for Palermo. You'll be welcome to the ride."

"What happens to you at Palermo?"

"I fly to England." He very nearly added: "All good things come to an end," but instead he shrugged and substituted: "Work—there's no escape from it for long."

"Shouldn't I stay for the funeral?"

40

"That's up to you, but the police are checking with the next-of-kin, which means there may be some delay about funeral arrangements. Anyhow, you needn't decide here and now. There will be a spare seat right up to the moment I leave." After a few seconds he added: "You won't be deserting Frank, you know. You've got to be thinking about yourself, Inger—what's best, what's most sensible. And surely the most sensible thing is to put yourself in the hands of your Consul?... Wouldn't Frank be the first to agree to that?"

His father might have been talking—"Diana's dead, Neal. Face up to it, brutal though it is. You did everything a man could. My God, you almost went too. Be practical. Concentrate on yourself. There's no other way, believe me ..."

Forrester gazed at the girl, wondering whether remorse was troubling her at all, whether she had asked herself if Nolan might conceivably be alive but for her. But there was a quality of innocence about her face that disarmed such an idea. Anyhow, he thought dismissively, what's it to me? He was calling her by name, but they were strangers still, and strangers they'd remain even if he took her across the island to Palermo. And that would be it: even the Good Samaritan had moved on.

The dream returned to him that night, the self-same merciless dream, but only a fraction of it, the climax, the part where the shale started giving under his feet, scattering over Diana as she clung to the angle of cliff, one arm stretched towards his, sobbing breath, fingers reaching, and then his feet no longer getting any purchase, sliding, stamping, and Diana's eyes from only a few feet away, every second elongated into frantic lengths of time, and then the shale suddenly going down in a gritty slithering wave, taking her with it in a great sucking yawn of noise while he watched.

When the dream woke him, as it always did, Forrester lay

41

cold in the bed, hounded again across the years by the recollection. It was five o'clock and he got up, put on his dressing-gown and went in slippers on to the veranda. An hour later he was still there, smoking, watching the pink and pewter dawn beginning to make the new day as the world turned.

8

HE took breakfast in his room. Soon after nine the switchboard rang through with a message from the police post—would he and Miss Lindeman please report there between ten and eleven o'clock? Forrester got the operator to connect him with Number 47.

"Inger?"

"Yes . . . Oh, it's you."

"Are you dressed?"

"Half and half." Disembodied, her accent seemed more marked.

"The police want to see us this morning—before eleven. Can we meet downstairs in an hour or so?"

When she came she was wearing a white linen costume; it was the one and only time her wardrobe showed evidence of further variety. They walked to the police post in the April sunshine, to be shown on arrival into the same office as before with its cloying cigar-smoke pungency and the blatant, libidinal gaze of its occupant.

"*Buon giorno, signorina . . . signore.*"

No one else was there. An anonymous civic dignitary stared at them from a frame askew on the wall. They sat down and

42

waited while the officer shuffled some papers. Perhaps he was trying to give the impression of overwork, or of having innumerable and pressing responsibilities. Fussing, he eventually found what he wanted.

"Ah yes," he wheezed, leaning back and glancing quickly at the girl's legs under the desk. "The doctor's report . . ." He cleared his throat, then addressed Forrester. "It says here that the dead man had a heavy concentration of sodium amytal in his system. It also says, in effect, that there was no evidence of cardiac or arterial weakness and that no other cause of death can be attributed."

"He killed himself, in fact," Forrester said.

"It will be for the inquest to rule whether the dose was self-administered—"

"Oh, to blazes."

Surprisingly, the officer nodded. "I agree with you. The circumstances point to it being so. All I am saying is that it is not for me to make the official pronouncement."

Forrester thought he detected a hint in the button eyes. "But you already know what that pronouncement will be?"

"You could say so, yes."

"Suicide?"

A nod. "You could say so."

They did things differently here. The ceiling-fan fluttered the ends of the weighted papers on the officer's desk.

"Inform the *signorina* of the situation, please," he said. "Tell her, if you will, that for her peace of mind I am taking her into my confidence."

He seemed anxious to win gratitude from her, recognition, God knows. It must be hard, Forrester thought, to lust so hungrily and to be totally ignored. On both visits she had hardly even looked at him.

"For her peace of mind," he repeated. "This is advance information. Private."

43

Forrester told her, but not as a favour.

"She is relieved, I am sure," the officer suggested hopefully.

"Relieved?"

"To know that there will be no complications for her. No trouble."

"Hasn't she had trouble enough?"

The officer spread his arms like an angler. *"Signore,* you misunderstand. It could have been worse for her. More difficult. That is what I am saying."

"It will make everything easier if she has her passport back."

"Of course. I have it here, waiting." Like many fat men he was nimble on his feet. He went to one of the filing-cabinets, stomach held in, and found the passport. "Here," he said, making a point of giving it personally to the girl, going round behind her, able to touch her at last, hand excusably on shoulder. "With my compliments, *signorina.* A pleasure."

She asked Forrester: "What did he say?"

"He's telling you you're free to go." To the officer he said: "The lady is grateful—most grateful." Smarmy bastard. "Has Nolan's next-of-kin been traced?"

"Headquarters are dealing with that, probably through his Consulate, and at present I do not know. Here we will act on the information provided—as regards family requests concerning the disposal of the body, for instance. And, of course, with foreigners, there are sometimes legal matters involved, such as debts and legitimate claims against the deceased's estate. Again, this is a Consulate concern. But Signorina Lindeman, fortunately for her, can be spared these tedious problems." Another lingering glance in her direction. "You can take it from me that she is at liberty to leave Sicily as and when she chooses."

Rising, Forrester told him: "She's probably travelling with me to Palermo."

"When will that be?"

44

"Tomorrow."

"Ah." With reluctance the officer moved to the door; given a chance he would have prolonged the small talk, the proximity. "Well, I wish you both a pleasant journey." Enviously he again smiled the parting smile which inferred that he also was a man of the world. "Good-bye, *signore* . . . *signorina*." And Forrester felt his eyes on their backs as he and Inger walked along the corridor.

9

S HE came with him next day. Someone on the other side of the world had a claim on Nolan—mother, father, sister, brother; maybe a wife—and it wasn't for Inger to elect what became of his sewn-up, refrigerated corpse. Not that she expressed any views. Tuesday morning remained for her the ultimate finality and she could cope with nothing else, though she left four thousand *lire* with the hotel manager to be spent on roses if Nolan was buried in Taormina—a generous sum considering what remained when her bill was settled. In a way it seemed the sentimental gesture of a child. "Should I stay?" she'd asked Forrester a second time, and he'd answered much as before: "Not unless you feel you must." For what? He was neither being unfair on her nor sitting in moral judgment, but only the heart clings achingly to the last—and Nolan could hardly have sought, or entered, her there.

Yes, he reckoned Nolan would diminish. Taormina itself was already a memory. In a matter of hours they had entered a wilderness. The most recent signpost had crooked a broken

45

metal finger towards the sky, but whatever name and distance it proclaimed were all but eaten away by rust and Forrester hadn't spared it more than a glance. Then as now there was no choice of route, then as now he could see the solitary road snaking along the scrawny hills like a frayed chalk-line. But presently, after several empty miles, he asked: "Where's next?"

He couldn't risk taking his eyes off the road for more than a second or so. The girl had a map between them on the seat, but she was no navigator.

"Leonforte," she said without conviction.

"Is that a suggestion or a fact?"

"Provided we have passed Agira."

"Agira's where I nearly had that dog under us."

"Oh ... Well, it will be Leonforte."

"I could do with a drink. Aren't you parched? I'm as dry as a bone."

Back in Taormina the manager had said: "Why that way to Palermo, *signore*? Why not go to Capo d'Orlando and then along by the sea through Cefalú and Términi? A better road, more interesting places. And quicker. No? ... Well, it is up to you—naturally." This with the lift of the shoulders of one who knows best. "But inland you will find another kind of Sicily. *Antipatico*. Nothing but hills."

He wasn't entirely accurate. Once in a while a village showed in the heaped-up distance like a patch of bird-droppings, now and again a river glittered through the haze of heat and shabby farm-buildings huddled in the serpentine floor of a valley. But the almond-trees and cypresses along the littoral, the carnations and lemon groves and the multicoloured plaster walls straight out of the travel brochures belonged where the silver-white beaches were—behind Etna. This was stark, savage country, the road often like a shelf with unnerving gorges sheer on its open side.

46

The 1800 Fiat handled well. All morning Forrester had driven with care, wrestling the wheel on the endless curves as the road bucked and twisted around Etna's huge base, spreading a long trail of dust over the high desolation where they now found themselves. Hardly another car shared it with them, only an occasional truck, sometimes a lonely man plodding along the verge or gazing down at them from a rocky slope with goats moving amid the scrub and prickly pear. A different Sicily, all right, wild beyond Forrester's imagination, and one that he'd never have seen if he'd allowed the manager to route them. Yet Palermo was still within comfortable reach; they'd be there by evening.

He sounded the horn and the tyres whimpered through yet another S-bend. Then the road ran straight for a while, with a plunging fall-away to their left. A few gauzy slicks of high cloud, eroded outcrops of yellow rock on the steep bare hillside ahead, no evidence of human activity—until, at last, Leonforte showed. For the passer-by it was a nondescript town, small and compact, clustered above vineyards and patches of gnarled olive smallholdings with tight streets and sunless back alleys to nowhere. Forrester parked the car in the main square and he and Inger crossed to a café where chequer-board tables stood beneath some plane trees. She ordered Cinzano-soda and Forrester a beer. The trees shook their shadows gently in the sun and the waiter departed with his metal tray, plucking morosely at a frayed cuff.

Forrester stretched his legs. "D'you feel like eating?"

"Here?"

"God forbid. Unless you're ravenous I thought we could push on to Enna, or even to Caltanissetta. What d'you say?"

"I can wait."

Their drinks came, cold and slaking. Forrester drained his and ordered another. The girl was almost beautiful in the dappled light, her hair brown, nothing false about her face;

the pallor had gone and the tan glowed. She was wearing the trousers from the blue suit but jacketless now, with a sleeveless white cotton sweater.

They were alone for barely ten minutes before a black-shawled woman came to beg. Forrester gave her some small change and she moved away; none of the other tables was occupied. Then a youth arrived, bird-like in his movements, confiding, bending close at Forrester's elbow; he seemed to materialise out of nowhere.

In sibilant English he said: "Watch, sir? Want good watch?"

"No."

"Very cheap."

"No."

"Swiss watch. Twenty-five thousand *lire*."

"No."

He bent closer, like a pornographer, lowering his voice. "For lady?"

"No."

"Only twenty thousand *lire*."

In exasperation, Forrester's eyes met Inger's. "No," he said forcibly. "Go away, for God's sake."

"Special price for lady. Fifteen thousand *lire*. Swiss watch, very very pretty. Look—I show." In a flash it was on the table, its worn tissue wrapping peeled off. "Gold. Made in Swiss."

"Gold, nothing."

"Gold, yes. Many jewels." Quick fingers slid the watch across the table. "The lady like?"

Inger didn't move. But again her indifferent eyes met Forrester's and Forrester said: "They're devils, aren't they?" Then, to the man: "We aren't interested. You're wasting your time."

"Time?... Yes, yes—good time. Swiss."

"Go away."

"Fourteen thousand? . . . For lady? Pretty watch for pretty lady."

"Clear off!" At last Forrester let fly in Italian. "Get the hell out of here—and hurry."

A wounded shrug. *"Signore—"*

"Fa presto!"

The youth snatched up the watch and went, one more defeat under his belt. Forrester reached for his beer. "They're so damned persistent," he muttered with a shake of his head.

"When Frank said no," Inger remarked, "that was the end of it"—and to Forrester it sounded like an accusation.

10

ETNA was still there sometimes even now, quivering distantly in the rear-view mirror. They were climbing again, the panoramas widening, the land more hostile, if possible, than before. About five miles out of Leonforte a series of hairpins demanded all Forrester's concentration, but when the road levelled off he opened the throttle; surprisingly Inger's remark niggled. It wasn't long after midday and the dust curdled behind them under the brassy sun. Cactus by the wayside, thorn bushes, rock and coarse scrub; either that or dramatic gorges with far-off glimpses of cultivation and perhaps a big house centred amid disciplined concentrations of green.

Ahead, the road split left and right by a wayside call-box.

49

Nearing the fork Forrester could see two men, one in the centre of the road, one sitting by the bank. The one in the centre started waving, legs apart, facing towards them; even at fifty yards his teeth showed in a grin.

"What the hell—?"

Forrester braked. The man held his ground, arms raised as if in surrender. The grin didn't falter. Not until the Fiat had come to rest within feet of him and the following wave of dust was drifting over did he move; then he skipped round to Forrester's side.

"*Inglese?*"

"*Sì.*"

"*Parla l'italiano?*" Dark blue suit, grubby cream shirt, no tie; thin, thongy wrists.

"*Sì.* What d'you want?"

"My brother has hurt his leg. His ankle."

The one on the bank acknowledged Forrester's glance with a moody nod. He was the younger of the pair—twenty-ish, and rougher looking. Both were very swarthy.

"Where are you making for?" Forrester said, cutting the engine.

"Caltanissetta." The man by the car really had the most ferocious grin. It was like a permanent fixture; but above it the eyes were sharp and darting. "Not far for you."

"You're in luck. Climb in."

"*Tante grazie.*" Then, over his shoulder: "*Va bene, Guiseppe.*"

The brother hobbled over and they clambered into the rear seat. Forrester watched them in the mirror: country boys.

"How did you hurt your ankle?"

"On a stone up there. I twisted it." He was gruff and surly. And yet on edge; Forrester could sense his tension.

"We were taking a short cut," the first one grinned.

"English?" the brother asked, obviously in doubt.

50

"English—yes."

"You speak good Italian."

"Thanks."

Forrester switched on. As he did so the brother asked a curious thing. "Esso?"

Forrester had filled up in Taormina, though for the life of him he couldn't remember with what. Carelessly, he nodded, shifting into gear and releasing the handbrake. "That's right."

"Your wife is beautiful," the other one remarked after a pause.

Forrester smiled back at the grin. To Inger he said: "They're being complimentary about you."

She didn't respond. He drove a quarter of a mile or so in silence. Presently there was a solid, metallic-sounding click which he couldn't place. Glancing into the mirror again he saw the man behind him lean forward; then he felt a jacket-sleeve against his neck-hair as an arm rested on the top of the seat. For half a moment Forrester imagined he was about to be offered a cigarette.

"*Signore*—we are not going to Caltanissetta."

"No?" Even then he hadn't grasped that something might be wrong. "Where, then?"

"I will show you. It is not on this road."

"Sorry, but I'm not making any detours."

"You are." The voice was very quiet, almost against his neck, but its intensity carried a built-in threat: the manner of address had suddenly changed to the familiar and disdainful *tu*.

"Now look here—" Forrester began.

Slowing, he half turned in his seat. And then, with a chill of alarm, he saw that the man was pointing an automatic pistol at him.

. . . . .

Inger must have seen it simultaneously: Forrester was vaguely aware of her startled gasp. But for seconds on end the gun seemed to have him mesmerised. He flung a glance at the road, meaning to draw into the side.

"Don't stop!"

"Listen—"

"Keep going—I'm warning you."

"Do as he says," the other one grated.

Forrester held the car at low speed. "Is this a game? Some kind of a game?"

"No game."

"Who are you?"

"Do as I tell you and neither of you will be hurt."

"Who are you?"

"Carlo and Guiseppe—brothers."

"What's this all about?"

"You'll see."

Now Inger: "What is happening? Who are they?" She was scared, pressing against the door.

"God knows."

"What do they want?"

Over his shoulder Forrester said: "*Cosa vogliono?* . . . Money?"

"Everyone wants that"—this with a snigger.

"I have some money."

"But of course. . . . Now, I suggest you drive faster."

A prod between the shoulder-blades. The film of sweat on Forrester's neck and forehead felt icy. Reluctantly he increased the speed: the verge blurred past.

"What do they want?" Inger repeated.

"They haven't said."

"Ask them."

"What d'you think I've been doing?"

He shot her a sidelong glance, anger in his alarm, thoughts

jumping in all directions. To the rear he gritted: "Where are we going?"

"You'll see."

Forrester licked his lips. "Wherever it is you'll regret this."

"Listen to him," one said to the other. "*Cane mordace.*" And chuckled.

The road dipped, climbed and twisted. A warning horn suddenly blared and Forrester hugged the side on two blind corners in succession. On the third the horn sounded again, close, and a blue-and-chrome coach swung round the turn. Forrester braked sharply to give it room. A score of tourists gazed down at them as it edged past, cocooned in their contentment, and helplessly he watched them go, hearing with a kind of disbelief the guide with the hand-microphone saying: "You cannot see it from here, ladies and gentlemen, but ten kilometres to your right is Lake Pergusa, near which, according to legend, Pluto carried off Proserpine . . .' Nightmares were made of incidents like this.

No sooner had the coach disappeared in its own dust than Forrester realised he had missed his chance: if he'd pulled across the path of the coach, rammed its side even, then the gun behind him would have been useless. As it was it crippled every prospect of refusal or escape. Next time, he thought feverishly . . . Coaches were rare, but there might be a truck or another car; witnesses. Something could be done. The coach had come too soon, catching him unprepared for action. Next time, though . . . He tensed expectantly, on the lookout, sounding his own horn in the hope of hearing another answer.

But there was no next time. The road was all theirs, and remained so for minutes on end. Then a sign-post pointed left to Enna and he was told to filter away to the right. The surface under them vanished; they were on a rocky track and on either side it might have been the pock-marked surface of the moon.

Forrester began again, bewildered, uncomprehending, still thinking in terms of robbery. "If it's money you want—"

"Just keep driving." Dark aggressive eyes met his in the vibrating mirror. "There will be time enough for talk."

"What are you saying?" Inger cut in.

"They won't answer any questions."

"What are you going to do?"

"What *can* I do?" Something in her look made him snap: "I've no choice, have I?" Don't tell me, he fumed, what Nolan would have done. But that part died on his tongue.

11

THEY must have covered a dozen crunching miles from the road-and-track junction. Time and again pot-holes reduced Forrester almost to a crawl.

"This isn't my car," he tried once more. "It's rented"—as if there was a measure of deterrent in the fact. But it drew no comment from the back.

They were high now, as high as they'd been all day, with unknown villages embattled in the heat-discoloured distances. Yet here and for miles around there was nothing—neither cultivation nor habitation, at most a few broken stone-piled walls like abandoned defence positions. But when they descended into the depressions that lay in uneven succession across the line of the track the world closed tight around them as the skyline rose. Conifers filled most of these long hollows, and once they crossed the dried-up bed of a stream, bleached wood like bones littered along its rocky channel.

It was beginning to seem to Forrester that he couldn't remember a time when he hadn't driven with the knowledge of a gun behind him and the reflections of the two Sicilians' faces as proof of its existence. He'd never felt so powerless for so long. "Another kind of Sicily up there, *signore*"—the hotel manager's words echoed like a taunt. "*Antipatico.*"

"What are you?—*mafiosi?*"

The grin flashed again. "If we were, would we say?"

Forrester swore at them. Guiseppe, the one with the bogus limp, coloured and jerked forward, but the brother restrained him. "Easy, easy. You know what Salvatore said." Then he tapped Forrester on the shoulder. "Go left over this next rise. Slow down a little—the turn comes quite soon."

The Fiat crested the incline. Another deep hollow confronted them, thick with pines.

"Here," Carlo ordered, pointing. "Turn here."

Forrester swung on to a dirt path. Water flowed in a gully beside it. The path lost its identity, but it was still possible to thread a way through the trees. Sunlight splintered overhead and they went a flickering half-mile or so before reaching a small clearing where a low rectangular stone building stood at the base of some enormous boulders. It was little more than a hut. Water was spilling in a thin silvery cord over the face of a rocky bluff and the boulders were green with moss.

"Stop now."

The car rocked to a halt. There was a movement at one of the hut's windows.

"Go tell him, Guiseppe."

"*D'accordo.*" He jog-trotted away, no limp now.

Carlo motioned with the gun. "Both of you."

"They want us out," Forrester told Inger.

The ground was springy underfoot; they walked without noise, Carlo behind. The sound of the waterfall stressed the encasing silence. Guiseppe had already disappeared into the

55

building but he emerged with another man, middle-aged, thickset, in shirt-sleeves.

"*Rallegramenti, Carlo!* So you got your fish." Advancing, the newcomer came with his thumbs dug behind a heavy belt. Hook nose, grey showing in the black hair and the palest eyes Forrester had ever seen, practically colourless. The square face was very lined, the cheeks hollow.

He gave a mock bow. "I am told you speak Italian."

"I do, yes." Forrester said. "And I want to know what the hell you and your friends imagine you're playing at."

"I should have thought that was obvious."

"Not to me it isn't."

"You have been kidnapped." The man seemed amused. His voice was deep, the dialect pronounced. "What other explanation could there be? And we are not playing—that I can assure you." To Carlo he said: "Take the car round to the back." He commanded respect; Carlo moved obediently. "Nice car."

"Why should you want to kidnap us?"

"Ah, now that is complicated. We must talk about it."

"Now."

"Now if you wish. But inside." He motioned to them to precede him. Almost apologetically he warned Forrester: "Do not attempt anything rash. You and your wife wouldn't get far. And our wish is that neither of you should be harmed."

Forrester took Inger by the arm. As they walked he said: "I'm still in the dark. But don't worry. We'll be all right." He was more uncertain than he tried to sound.

"What do they want? Who are they?"

Nerves were making her repeat herself. He could feel the goose-flesh against his fingers; perhaps she would have been less frightened if she had had some glimmering of the language. With difficulty he realised that it must have been worse for her.

56

"That's what I intend to find out."

There were three sagging board steps up to the door. They entered a room in which was little except a battered pine table and a few rough chairs; three doors led off and there was a sink at one end with a bucket standing on the draining-board. Alongside was a stove, its rickety flue-pipe poking up through the low roof. The remains of a meal—glass, dirty plate and fork—was at one end of the table with a half-empty bottle of red wine. The floor was of stone and light came from two windows, sacking draped crudely at their sides.

"A chair for the *signora*, Guiseppe. We must make our guests as comfortable as possible."

Forrester remained on his feet. "You were going to give us an explanation."

"Certainly."

"Well?"

"Sit down," the senior man said. He must be the one the others called Salvatore. He pulled back a chair for himself. "It will take a little time. Guiseppe, some wine for the *signora*."

Impatiently, Forrester joined him at the table. "Listen—I'm a British subject and this lady—"

"We know exactly who you are."

"Nonsense."

"It is precisely because we know who you are that you are both here."

"All right—who are we then?"

It came with quiet satisfaction. "You are George Russell—and this, of course, is your wife."

Forrester's eyes widened. "George *who*?"

"Russell." The pronunciation was extraordinary.

"Oh no, I'm not." With relief Forrester said to Inger: "They think we're someone else."

A momentary suspicion of the aside showed in Salvatore's

57

face. "We know who you are, and what you are, and where you spent last night."

"Tell me."

"You are General Manager for Esso and last night you and your wife stayed at the hotel in Leonforte."

"Esso?"

"Esso, yes."

Forrester smiled; it was so ridiculous. "You've got it all wrong, I'm afraid."

"Bluffing won't help. We know. And our intention is to ask the Esso Company for five million *lire* against your release."

So that was it. He'd once read a news-item about a similar ploy in Bolivia, perhaps Mexico.

"In which case, whoever you are, I'd better tell you something quick—otherwise you're going to make idiots of yourselves." Forrester began counting on his fingers. "One, my name is Forrester, not Russell. Two, this lady is a Norwegian citizen and she is not my wife. Three, I've nothing to do with Esso. And, four, last night Signorina Lindeman and I were at the Hotel Capua in Taormina."

Carlo entered the room just then; his grin began to fade as he listened.

"You were in Leonforte," Salvatore persisted, confidence not yet shaken. He clasped his hands, leaning forward.

"An hour ago, yes; but not last night."

The back of the wrists were tattooed. "You were in Leonforte, you are with Esso, and you drive a rented white 1800 Fiat."

"The Fiat's rented, yes. We passed through Leonforte, yes. But am I the Esso General Manager? No—most certainly I am not."

"You are lying." The mouth was a thin, taut line. Everyone lied.

"Unfortunately for you I'm telling the truth."

58

"Your name is George Russell."

"It is not."

"This is your wife."

"Wrong again." Forrester turned to Inger. "For some crazy reason they believe I'm a George Russell, that you're my wife, and that I'm in the oil business."

Salvatore rounded on her suspiciously. "What is he telling you?"

"You can ask her until you're blue in the face, but you won't get an answer. She doesn't speak a word of your language."

"What did you say to her?"

"That you're as wrong as wrong can be about us. I can very easily prove it. Our passports are in the car—"

Forrester rose, but Salvatore snapped: "Stay where you are. Carlo—get their luggage."

"My passport's in my jacket."

"Bring that, too. Bring everything."

Carlo went obediently, the swagger gone. On the other side of the room Guiseppe gestured uneasily from the wall.

"He told us he was with Esso. I asked him as soon as he picked us up and he confirmed it."

"I misunderstood you."

"You said you were with Esso."

"Oh, for God's sake! I thought you were asking what petrol I used."

A contemptuous roll of the eyes. "And you didn't deny the woman is your wife . . . He is lying, Salvatore."

"Of course he's lying," Salvatore growled. Then, reverting to Forrester: "We have a relative in Leonforte. Last night he confirmed where you were staying. This morning he reported your time of departure from the hotel." Forrester's expression must have made him add: "By telephone—there is a call-box at the junction where you were stopped."

59

"Then all I can say is that you shouldn't rely on relatives. This one's led you up the garden."

Salvatore felt the remark all over, looking for hidden meanings. His face darkened. "Don't provoke me, Signor Russell."

"For the last time—I am *not* Russell."

"We shall see about that."

"We'll see, all right."

Carlo clattered up the steps and backed in through the door: there were four cases in all—Inger's two, and Forrester's. He lugged them to the table and thudded them down. The jacket was bundled underarm and Forrester guessed he'd already examined the passport; he flashed a nervous glance in Guiseppe's direction that was part warning, part appeal. Forrester reached for his jacket as soon as it was heaped on the table, but Salvatore knocked his hand aside.

"What d'you take us for, eh?"

"I don't carry a gun, if that's what you're thinking."

A glare served as a reply. Salvatore found the correct pocket with the speed of a thief. "Now . . ." He narrowed his eyes as he drew out the passport and began turning the stiff pages; his lips moved as he peered to read a double spread of visa stamps.

"The particulars are at the front," Forrester told him.

"I know, I know."

Clearly he didn't, but he was vain; stubborn. When Forrester's photograph confronted him he stared at it and grunted. Then, laboriously, he worked over the opposite page, turned back to decipher more, the set of his face hardening as the truth gradually dawned. A vein swelled in his temples.

Finally he exploded: "Imbeciles!"

He flung the passport aside. His chair went over as he leapt to his feet. Carlo started to dart away but he grabbed him with the left hand and struck him a series of savage blows across the mouth with his right, jerking Carlo's head from side to side, raging abuse at him. Just as suddenly as he had begun he pushed Carlo clear and wheeled on Guiseppe.

"What kind of fools am I saddled with?" He went towards him. "D'you realise what you've done? . . . You, you useless—"

By the wall Guiseppe stiffened, flicking open a knife as Salvatore came to arm's length. "Try. Just try."

With astonishing swiftness the older man kicked at the extended wrist, sending the knife spinning, closing in with a flurry of knees and fists. Guiseppe sank to the floor, doubled up, hugging his stomach. Only a few seconds had elapsed.

"Even with a knife you are nothing," Salvatore snarled contemptuously. He spat. "Both of you are nothing." Carlo was leaning against the end of the table, blood trickling from his mouth. "God in Heaven, what chance has Angelo with lunatics for brothers? Do you know what you've done? . . . Do you? We wanted Russell, we planned for Russell, and you bring someone else . . . Someone else, do you hear?"

"It was a mistake," Carlo mumbled.

"*Madre di Dio!*"

"It was the only white Fiat to show—and the timing was right."

"Fool! Stupid, misbegotten fool!"

Inger and Forrester might not have been there. Forrester eyed Salvatore tensely. Antagonise him further, and there was no telling what his reaction would be. Move, and it might unite them all. Now, depending on what was said, and how it was said, everything would change. Across the table he saw Inger open her mouth, about to speak, in need of reassurance, an explanation—he could only guess—but he raised a finger to his lips, shaking his head.

"Excuses!" Salvatore raged on. "All you give me is excuses!"

He took a passing swipe at Carlo's head, which Carlo

61

ducked. Guiseppe still hugged himself on the floor, sullen in his pain.

"Woman!" Salvatore shouted down at him. "Woman, you."

His fury ebbed and flowed, violence followed by periods of blind swearing accompanied by enraged gestures. *"Merda!"* The glass and plate were swept away; the wine snatched up and gulped. *"Merda!"* At almost any other time it might have been comic. But he was unpredictable and dangerous; thwarted men were always dangerous, and this one believed himself cheated. Five million *lire* . . . Through no fault of his a dream had crumbled.

"Non è la mia colpa," he mimicked as Carlo mopped the blood. "Who was to blame, then? Tell me that—who?"

Suddenly he seemed to catch sight of Inger and Forrester again. And his anger changed course, as if he needed to prove that the others were as much sinned against as sinning. Such incompetence couldn't be true.

"You lied to the boys."

"No."

"You said you were Russell."

"Never."

"You didn't deny it."

"I wasn't asked."

"They were led to believe you were with Esso. Also that you are husband and wife."

"They assumed that."

For a moment Forrester thought Salvatore was about to strike him too.

"Who is she?"

"A friend."

"Where's her passport?"

Forrester asked Inger.

"The small case," he informed Salvatore. "It isn't locked. Look in the pocket in the lid."

This time the passport was given only brief examination. In disgust Salvatore tossed it on to the table. "*Christo!*" he said, and sucked in air, then ran his hands over his lined face.

Forrester waited, ill at ease. He was trying to be casual, yet casualness was out of place. All at once the falls sounded loud and clear, as if a breeze were playing tricks; but beyond the cracked and flyblown windows the pines stood motionless.

"Ask them about their own money," Guiseppe said, rising from the floor.

Salvatore turned to Forrester: "How much have you got?"

"Not the kind you're thinking of."

"How much?"

"Perhaps a hundred thousand."

Salvatore made an impatient gesture. "And the woman?"

"None."

"You expect me to believe that?" To possess a foreign passport, drive cars, put up in hotels, even second-class pensions— this, automatically, meant wealth.

"We're on our way home, so we're practically cleaned out. She might have two or three thousand left."

"The car could be sold," Carlo ventured. "Down in Agrigento, say. It's a million and a half *lire* car."

"And where are we then?—three and a half million short. *Madre!*" Salvatore might have been amongst enemies. "Use that apology of a head of yours. Think!"

Forrester stood up. "Listen," he said carefully. "You've got yourselves the wrong people. Signorina Lindeman and I are due in Palermo. She has urgent business with her Consul and I have a plane to catch." It sounded pretty lame, but a hard line was out of the question. "Most of what money there is is in travellers cheques, but you're welcome to the cash. So how about letting me have the car keys?"

Salvatore seemed taken aback. "Are you a fool like the others?"

63

"Maybe—though that's neither here nor there. But we do have a long journey and appointments to be kept."

"And people to inform."

"People?"

"The police."

"Certainly not. The incident's closed as far as we're concerned." Forrester could hear himself, like a parody of an Englishman at bay.

"For you perhaps, but not for me, not for us. Not necessarily."

"What d'you mean? We're no possible use to you, and—"

"Don't be so sure. Esso isn't the only whale in the sea." Salvatore moved closer, his face squeezed into a hundred lines. "What about your own company?"

"What about it?" Forrester stalled.

"Aren't you worth five million to your employers?"

"I shouldn't think so for one moment." Things were taking a different turn.

"Five million against your safe return . . . No?"

Prolonged self-control had never been Forrester's. "You're talking rubbish," he retorted sharply.

"Am I?"

"If you think you can raise that amount where I'm concerned you're as stupid as your two bone-headed friends are incompetent."

"*Insolente!* . . . What do you do? Just who are the two of you?"

"Find out."

Furiously, Salvatore started dragging everything from Inger's open case—shoes, underwear, brushes. She jumped from her chair—"No! . . . Please, no!"

"Lay off," Forrester shouted at him.

"You shut your mouth. Empty your pockets."

"Lay off, d'you hear?"

64

The situation was out of hand, he knew; but he wasn't expecting the blow. It came without warning and caught him hard on the underside of the jaw. And at once everything rocketed into darkness.

12

ONLY Inger was with him when he came round.
"Inger?" he said to the blur as light and shape took hold. Slowly he blinked her into focus. "Where are we?"
"They put us in this room."
Forrester winced as he raised his head. The place was about a dozen feet square. The rusted iron bedstead which he lay across was the only thing there. Sacking hung by the dirty windows, but the rest was as bare as a prison cell.
"How long was I out?"
"Out?"
"You know—gone."
"Right out—only a minute. Half out, two or three. They carried you in, then pushed me after."
He sat up, trying to regain his wits. His jaw felt twice its size. Voices murmured through the closed door.
"God, what a mess."
Inger said: "It is like . . . a nightmare for me."
"I can imagine."
"I'm scared," she said.
Twice now they had shared drama, and this time they were

equal partners. She sat beside him on the blanket which covered the bed, lips parted a little, eyes on his in appeal, in need of him. If she had been stone deaf the last hour could hardly have been more alarming. More than Nolan had receded; normality seemed a million miles away.

"Apparently they'd made plans to kidnap a Mr. and Mrs. Russell. Russell seems to be a senior man with Esso. He and his wife stayed in Leonforte last night and left this morning, about the time we did. A colleague of theirs kept them notified—by phone, they say." Gingerly, Forrester massaged his chin. "It so happens the Russells are also driving a white Fiat, but as luck would have it we were the ones who got to that junction first—and that was enough."

"Who are these men?"

"Thugs? Bandits?" Forrester humped his shoulders resentfully. He was sure they weren't *mafiosi*; the *mafiosi* saw themselves as an *élite*, but these people lacked any aura of power. "If we're any example to go by they're blundering amateurs, but they've set their sights high. They were banking on five million *lire* from the Esso Company, and as far as I can make out it's a set figure. Don't ask me why. The one who hit me—Salvatore—wasn't talking in terms of settling for anything less. For some reason five million is what they're after."

Inger frowned. "From us?"

"They'll be lucky!" Well over three thousand pounds. "My company isn't in a position to cope with a demand of that kind. We aren't an international set-up; and in any case we're subject to all manner of foreign exchange restrictions." He was thinking aloud, oblivious of whether she followed him or not. "Besides—"

"Will they keep us here?"

Forrester moved from the bed and examined both windows. They were freshly barred on the outside.

"They certainly intended keeping the Russells."

"But what can they get from us?"

"Not much—though they have to be convinced of that."

The voices crescendoed in the other room; they were still licking their wounds.

"I am bad luck." Where exactly Inger's mind was then Forrester couldn't tell, but she was suddenly distraught.

"Don't say that."

"It is true." She brushed hair from her face with a kind of hopelessness. "True."

"I'm partly to blame," Forrester said. "I wasn't very clever just now."

"You tried."

Strangely he was flattered. In his anxiety he turned his attention to the windows again. If he dwelt on it he knew he could fear for her; for them both. Somehow he had to get them out of here, but argument seemed to be his only weapon—argument, and one perhaps persuasive lie.

13

TEN minutes passed before a key grated in the lock and Salvatore opened the door.

"Have you cooled off?" He paused as though acknowledging Forrester's enmity. "Come, there is more talking to do."

Forrester followed him into the other room, humiliation only a part of what he felt. All the suit-cases had been emptied, their contents spread over the long table. He had expected this, though the sight galled him further, renewing the instinctive urge to remonstrate. Somehow he beat it down. Whatever rights Inger and he might have believed were theirs had vanished the moment Carlo and Guiseppe got into the Fiat; but only now had it sunk in.

Salvatore fixed his pale stare on him. "What connection have you with the police?"

"No connection at all."

"There are police entries in your passports. In them both."

"That's because of an investigation in Taormina. They stamped the passports."

"Why?"

"Habit? . . . You should ask them."

"What kind of investigation was this?"

"Signorina Lindeman's companion died. She and I were questioned."

"And—?"

"And nothing. They were making routine enquiries. I was involved primarily as interpreter. After the enquiries were completed I offered to drive her to Palermo. She's had a bad time," he added, and it was as near to an appeal as he came. That wasn't the way.

Salvatore grunted, apparently satisfied. "Now," he said, back to square one, "I want to hear about this company of yours."

"There is no company."

"No company? You have no employer?"

"I work for myself."

"Where?"

"In England."

"Where in England?"

"Peterborough."

Salvatore frowned. His gaze moved briefly to Carlo, who stood behind Forrester, then away.

"Spell that place."

"Spell it?"

"Spell it, yes."

Forrester did so, rubbing his jaw.

"And you belong to no company?"

"I told you." All his suppressed anger was welling up again. "I'm self-employed. There's no one for you to bargain with, no one to tap. You got the wrong man."

"This time I know for sure you are lying."

"You keep saying that."

Salvatore gestured, as if he were tossing a ball. "Show him the address, Carlo."

Carlo moved to Forrester's elbow and thrust a business card into his hand. It was immediately recognisable and Forrester's heart sank. He could have kicked himself. The card must have been loose in one of his cases, or in a side pocket, forgotten.

Neal J Forrester, M.C.

STONE AND FORRESTER LIMITED

PETERBOROUGH

DEMOLITION CONTRACTORS

"You see, *signore*?" A hard, mirthless smile that hollowed the cheeks even deeper.

"It's misleading. I'm no longer with that company."

"Your own name is part of the company's name."

"So?"

"You expect me to believe that this is a coincidence?"

"It's a common enough name."

"When did you leave?"

"Some time ago."

"Years? ... Months?"

"Years. Two years."

"Then why do you also carry an up-to-date diary belonging

69

to these people—with your own initials printed on the outside?"

Forrester shrugged. Suddenly it seemed futile to go on.

"All right, it is my company. But it's no Esso. We're a very small concern. *Spicciolo*. What I'm trying to tell you is that you haven't a chance of raising five million *lire* from that quarter. Not a chance."

As he spoke he had a forward flash of how it might be, with his father saying in that gruff disapproving way of his: "How, in God's name, could you get mixed up with people like that? Really, Neal, it's too bad. And who was this woman? . . ." The world had hardly touched his father; so much of it was improper, and what was improper was avoidable. The stepping-stones which had led Forrester here would never have been his. If Nolan had died in the adjoining bedroom he'd have called the doctor and the manager, then gone downstairs for breakfast. So there would have been no involvement with Inger, no feeling of responsibility, no kidnap on the road, no stone hut in the back of beyond, no three men, no gun, no knife, no hollow-cheeked insistence on money. Chance worked differently for his father. And in testy complaint he would say: "Your life's your own, Neal. But it beats the band that you should expect Stone and Forrester to bail you out . . ."

All this a thousand times faster than speech.

"Let me ask you a question," Forrester went on quickly. "Why five million? Why not settle for what you've got and call it a day?"

"It has to be five million."

"Why?"

"Because less will not be enough. And we need it soon."

"How soon?"

"Within a week."

"You haven't a hope. With Esso, maybe. They'd have funds locally. But my company—even if it were able to oblige, which

70

it isn't—would probably need twice that long to get approval to the transfer, and there's no guarantee of its being forthcoming."

To Forrester's surprise he wasn't interrupted. He'd hardly expected a chance to reason, but he began to speak about the restrictions imposed by the Treasury, stressing the difficulties, the limitations, the impersonal level of decision. His cousins in Rome had helped as usual with some *lire* on the side—otherwise he'd never have been able to squander as much as he had at roulette—but he kept them out of it. Companies, corporations, individuals—everyone back home, he told Salvatore, was in the same boat.

"You might wait a month, and then be turned down. You can't shove a pistol into someone's back over there."

All the signs were that Salvatore was at least unsettled. Restlessly he moved about the room. Once he swatted the air angrily and swore. Guiseppe and Carlo stayed well clear, watching him; Guiseppe, the knife retrieved, was picking his nails. For a short while Forrester believed he had at last planted a seed of doubt; indeed, he glanced towards Inger, trying to convey that Salvatore might finally have realised he had bitten off something not worth chewing.

But then Salvatore said: "This company of yours—what does it make?"

"We don't."

"Explain."

Forrester did so, off guard, relieved by Salvatore's uncertainty. 'Demolition contractors' made clumsy wording in Italian.

"What do you demolish?"

"Pretty well anything—it depends. On land, under water. Buildings, towers, wrecks . . ."

"What do you use?"

"Again it depends."

71

"Explosives?"

"Explosives, yes," Forrester nodded.

Salvatore suddenly gripped Forrester fiercely on the shoulders, nails digging deep, his face creasing with excitement. Then he spun on the others. "Did you hear? . . . Did you? Miracles hapen even now, *ragazzi*. Miracles, I tell you. We have landed a dynamiter." And he burst into laughter.

14

H E was still laughing when someone clattered up the steps and the outer door opened. Another man came in, younger than either Carlo or Guiseppe, handsome, with sleek finger-waved hair. He nodded with satisfaction when he saw Inger and Forrester.

"So—it worked."

"*Ciao*," Carlo said. "You've taken your time."

"It was an hour before I could thumb a ride." He bent to beat dust from his tight trousers and pointed shoes. "I see you and Guiseppe got yours."

"But in the wrong car"—this, with relish from Salvatore.

"*Impossible!*"

"The wrong car, with the wrong people."

"No!"

"Yes, Luigi, *yes* . . . For which fiasco you are as much to blame as your no-good brothers. Didn't you notice another white Fiat in Leonforte?"

"Another? . . . I was near the hotel, only near the hotel."

"In which case you think the Russells look like these two?"

Luigi's gaze returned in dumbfounded silence to Inger and Forrester. He feared Salvatore; they all did, and it showed along with the dismay.

"Well?"

"I . . . I'm not sure," he faltered.

"Not sure!" Salvatore mocked. "*Christo!*"

"I never saw them close to. I have this friend on the staff; he kept me informed. I couldn't hang about inside the place."

"I am surrounded by incompetents," Salvatore stormed, and struck his fist against his forehead. But his anger was simulated. He was playing Luigi cat and mouse, enjoying his discomfiture. "However, perhaps all is not lost. By chance—and no thanks to any of you—we have a dynamiter in our midst." Again he laughed. "An explosives expert. What d'you say to *that*?" And he clapped his hands together.

Forrester took a pace towards him. "Just what is this? What are you getting at?"

"All in good time."

From across the room Guiseppe began: "Do you mean—?"

"Have I always to explain everything to you?"

"No, but—"

"Have we got the Russells—no we have not. Will we get the five million—no we will not. But what have we got instead— the possibility of an alternative. Don't you see? Is your skull that thick?"

Guiseppe flashed him an ugly look. "I see," he said in a surly voice. "But you might as well suggest we climb Etna on our hands. We wouldn't have a hope."

"You're wrong."

"Such a thing could never work."

"It must. *Must.*"

"What must?" Forrester snapped. "For God's sake—"

Salvatore hadn't finished with the others. "Face the facts.

73

There *is* no other way, not as things are. We are left with this, this or nothing, and to do nothing would be a crime." He turned to Forrester. "And you will help us."

"You're talking in riddles. But if you imagine I'm going to be party to blowing a bank or something of the sort you're out of your mind."

"It's not a bank."

"Whatever it is."

Salvatore's eyes flashed. "Listen," he said, the mouth hard again. "We picked you up in good faith, thinking you were someone else, someone we could use as a lever, someone who would help to open doors. The error was ours, but fortunately errors are not always disastrous. Those doors can still be opened—and you will make it possible."

"And if I refuse?"

"You won't refuse."

"I damned well will. Just who the hell do you suppose you are?"

Salvatore prodded with a finger. "You may find this hard to believe, but—speaking personally—I wish you no harm, either of you. But your safety is of minor importance to me and the boys compared with what is at stake. Let me put it this way. Both of you have already disappeared; already you have been taken out of circulation—and no one is the wiser. Whether or not your disappearance is to be made permanent will be for you to decide." An entire world of indifference was in the way he spread his hands. "I am sorry, but there it is."

Forrester glanced desperately at Inger, then back to Salvatore, the others all watching, as still as statues. His voice shook. "You wouldn't dare."

"Oh yes"—very quietly, with a nod. "If need be."

There was a long silence: ash shifted in the stove.

"We aren't in this place for our health," Salvatore went on. "Perhaps you should know a little about our background if

74

you doubt my sincerity. Someone was killed; a fool of a police-man. All of us are on the wanted list—all, that is, except one."

"I don't understand."

"There are four brothers. Three are present here, the fourth —Angelo—is in the Monteliana jail. Five million *lire* would have got him out; a price had been negotiated for his escape." Salvatore darted an unforgiving glance at the others. "Even so it was always a gamble whether we could raise the money from Esso in time. So now, friend, we will gamble another way. We will pick your brains about explosives instead, and you will show us how to get Angelo out of there ourselves." He waited, studying Forrester clinically. "It is unfortunate for you, but you have no choice, no choice at all. Think it over—and, in case you imagine you are in a bargaining position, remember this. We are going to need you, but we don't need the woman. And I suggest the knowledge of that will guarantee your co-operation."

15

FROM the beginning there had never been more than three possibilities open to Forrester—force, bribery and persuasion. All had died in turn. Yet from the moment he realised that he and Inger were the victims of chance and error he hadn't seriously doubted the almost unbelievable charade would come to a satisfactory end before the day was out. He thought it certain they would be lighter by every *lire* and worthwhile possession in their luggage, but he had visualised an end to it none the less—until a few minutes ago. Between then and now a kind of madness had entered into Salvatore's thinking, a new ruthlessness that even the others didn't seem to realise might have been on its way. For a long-drawn second or two Forrester teetered on the brink of turning to them in appeal. His gaze swept them—Carlo with a nervous half-smile, Luigi rubbing the side of his face, Guiseppe moodily toying with the knife—and he knew that Salvatore would carry them with him. Fear, loyalty, honour—any or all of these must win: they would have honour of a kind.

Even so, he heard himself saying: "You can't be serious. You can't mean—"

"As sure as God made Christ, my friend, I mean it—every word."

"You're asking the impossible."

"Not if you weigh what is in the balance." Once in a while there was a smattering of education behind Salvatore's phrasing. "One death against our name speaks for itself, surely? We have nothing much to lose."

Clutching at straws now, Forrester blustered: "You've taken too much for granted. I haven't handled explosives in years."

"But you have knowledge of them—you admitted it."

"I'm not technically qualified. You're making a mistake if you're imagining that."

Salvatore thrust his hands into his belt, the tattoos showing: he wasn't to be rattled again. "If I were in your shoes I would have tried that one myself. But it won't work, not with me. Oh no. Back there in England I dare say you sit in a big chair at a big desk in a big office and always wear a fine suit and a white shirt and tell your men to go and do these demolitions." I know how it is, his raised shoulders said. "But if the worst came to the worst you could instruct others. And if you think you have forgotten—well, start refreshing your memory. You'll

76

have a little time. No one is rushing you. Nothing will happen today."

In vain Forrester looked for a hint of weakness in him, but there was none.

"Let the *signorina* go," he pleaded. "Let her take the car. I'll advise you if I must, but keep her out of this. She's suffered enough these past few days."

"She won't suffer any more unless you make it necessary."

"You're bluffing." Forrester was incredulous even now. Things like this happened to other people. "You must be bluffing."

"Do you want to chance it?" Salvatore paused, lips curling. "The choice is yours—but I cannot believe the *signorina* means so little to you."

Apprehensively Forrester moved his hands. "Afterwards—I want to know about afterwards."

"You will be of no interest to us afterwards."

"Meaning?"

"You can do what you like, go where you like—to the police if you wish. It won't matter then. We won't need you any more."

"What guarantee have I of that?"

"Guarantee? *Christo*, you expect guarantees?"

"I want to know."

" 'Afterwards' is another day, another time. We won't be here then. You will be free to do as you wish—you have my word on it."

"Your word?"

"My word, yes," Salvatore growled, his face like stone. "One does not need to be a *mafioso* to be a man of honour." He said this with a mixture of pride and contempt. "I have a nephew in Monteliana lock-up and his brothers and I have undertaken to get him out before he is transferred to the Ucciardone in Palermo and starts to rot his life away. Don't talk to me about

77

suffering, don't talk to me about injustice. My mother's milk was soured by these before I was weaned."

He turned aside as if his patience had gone. Forrester brushed past him and went to Inger. He had tried to shield her from so much, but within the last quarter-hour the situation had entered a new dimension, perilous and uncertain. And it was his fault. If only he'd held his tongue they would have been spared this. Inside himself he was raging.

"Come," he said. He led Inger by the arm through the open doorway into the small, barred room and shut the door.

16

"SIT down. I'll try and tell you."

She took the proffered cigarette and he lit it for her, then his own, fingers shaking slightly.

"We can't leave, can we?"

"No. What's happened is—"

"Do they still want money?"

"They want help instead."

"*Help?*"

"My help."

Forrester put it to her as best he could. He could understand her amazement; what he was saying sounded improbable even to himself. She started interrupting immediately, pressing for details, and he had none to give. He didn't even know where Monteliana was.

"Salvatore grabbed at the idea when he decided the ransom

thing was off. He took the others by surprise. There's no plan, nothing except the idea itself—and judging by Guiseppe's reaction it's lunacy. But Salvatore's set on it." Wearily, Forrester shook his head.

"How did they find out your business?"

"From that card of mine—remember?" He couldn't bear to tell her the entire truth. "I thought we might be on our way until then. I'd all but convinced him that five million was a dream he'd best forget—in fact I *did* convince him. Otherwise he wouldn't have latched on to this other thing . . ." He stopped, forehead puckered, staring blankly at the windows. Events had run away with them and his mind had barely kept pace.

"They can't make you help them."

He said nothing.

"You can refuse. Where would they be then?"

Either she had forgotten the violence or she supposed in some way that it would never go further, never reach out to include her. That Salvatore might have another lever, the ultimate pressure, didn't seem to have occurred to her.

"We'll be here for ever unless I do something . . . I've got my back to the wall, Inger—don't you see?"

Again he was filled with pity for her, though this time the emotion was like an extension of what he felt for himself. What did she expect of him? They had come a long way in three days, yet the barriers had never been more than partially lowered. They were as much apart now as when they'd lunched together that first time with Nolan hardly arrived at the morgue. All at once his isolation bore in on him. He slumped back on the bed, his mind swimming with despair. Through the door he heard Salvatore complain: "Where's Margherita? What's keeping her?" And dully it registered that there was yet another one of them.

. . . . .

As far as he could tell they weren't locked in; he didn't check nor did he re-examine the windows. There was no point. And for the time being he wanted to be alone with Inger, un-harried. He lay there thinking back, thinking forward, grappling with the sheer preposterousness of the situation, try-ing to get on terms with it, the endless lava flow of his thoughts occasionally spilling over into audibility.

Once he said: "It's monstrous, just bloody monstrous." And, later: "This can't happen . . . *Can't.*" Yet for the life of him he couldn't see what would stop it. Salvatore had already stamped on Guiseppe's objections, Salvatore whose eyes were sometimes filled with a fierce and chilling light. There was no chance of sowing discord. In the next room Salvatore was warming the others to his argument, now cajoling, now with contempt. For the most part the voices were muffled, yet their very persistence underlined the uselessness of Forrester con-tinuing to rack his brains. At one stage he reverted fretfully to the possibility of raising the money after all, only to discover that the arguments he'd used held water; at best they might get it, but never in time. That he should even consider this was another measure of his sense of defeat; Salvatore had the bit between his teeth and wasn't to be influenced again. Some-thing crude and desperate was on its way, and if the kidnap was any yardstick it would be dangerously ill-conceived. Sal-vatore spoke as if explosives were an automatic open sesame, a guarantee of success, and dread tightened around Forrester's heart as he wondered what the raid would entail, what de-cisions were being made for him. In protest and with a fleeting renewal of disbelief his mind stuttered that he was a tourist, a businessman; but he was as good as manacled to Salvatore's plans and he knew it.

He lay there, fingering his throbbing jaw. And Inger said: "Why must we be here for ever? They can't make you help them." She was sitting at the end of the bed, living her

80

own version of the nightmare, nervous and impatient at one and the same time. "Without you their hands are tied."

"I've no option."

"Why?"

Did she still suppose that Nolan could have refused?—Nolan who apparently had such a way with him. The dead became giants and others were measured against the legend.

"Because," Forrester answered with sudden spite, "they will kill us if I don't co-operate. It's as simple as that."

He watched the shock of it on her face—the lips quiver, the pupils momentarily transfix.

"Now d'you see?... I'm sorry," he said, "but you had to know."

He pushed himself up and went across the room. And not for the first time he told himself that the future might not have been so bleak if he had been on his own.

A new voice began to join with the others as he stood with his back turned. He went to the door and listened. "Did you have trouble?... *Ciao*, Margherita... What did you get?" The replies were brisk, the voice young. "What about you?" he heard. "What did *you* get?" And at once Salvatore took over, urgently, as if to placate her. "Everything's changed, but don't alarm yourself. We'll have Angelo out—quicker, maybe." She came back at him, cutting into his explanations; he seemed to be following her along the room. There was some confused talk which Forrester couldn't catch, three or four of them speaking at once, and when Salvatore again predominated he was being charitable. "What's done is done. Anyone could have made the mistake. But we aren't empty-handed... Yes, in there..." Forrester could almost see his gesture. "But listen, *ragazza*, listen. It might be worse. He is a dynamiter. A dynamiter, yes. We can break Monteliana open... But we can. We can. We have been going into it. The main gate, the cell window..."

A stifled sound from Inger drew Forrester back to her. "Don't," he said. "Please don't." He had no armour against tears. He moved in front of her and cupped her chin in his hands, tilting her face firmly towards his. "We'll be all right— honestly. Wait and see. We'll laugh about this one of these days . . . You know, visit beautiful Sicily and its friendly people." Singer, his company commander in Korea, had jollied him in self-same fashion the night before they moved into position. "Come on, Inger, snap out of it."

Oh Christ, he thought.

17

IT had gone four when Carlo opened the door. He was nothing if not resilient; his grin was fixed in place again with its awful lack of meaning.

"*Ha famé?*"

Forrester was famished; he hadn't eaten since a light break-fast.

"Hungry, Inger?" She showed no enthusiasm. "I shouldn't say no—God knows when we'll get anything else."

He went with her into the main room. He'd heard the scrape and clatter of plates during the last half-hour and now there was bread on the table, a saucepan of soup, some figs. Salvatore was already seated.

"Here is our dynamiter, Margherita."

She was at the sink, rinsing her hands in a bucket. She acknowledged them with her eyes only, gravely, first Forrester, then Inger. So many Sicilian women wore their hair tied severely back, but hers was loose, very dark against the olive skin, and the hard life showed in her features, more even than in Salvatore's; yet she must have been barely half his age. Black blouse, grey skirt, black woollen stockings—the dress was that of any village girl's.

"Margherita," Salvatore said with evident pride, "is Angelo's wife. She is also a fine cook." He indicated the empty chairs. "Come and see. *Sì accommodi.*"

Forrester sat beside Inger. He was too hungry to care about sharing the table with the rest of them, but Inger met their glances with self-conscious defiance. Carlo was on Forrester's right, Guiseppe and Luigi opposite, Salvatore at one end. They helped themselves from the saucepan, filling their bowls in turn; the thin, garlic-laced soup contained pellets of pasta and traces of stringy meat.

"Join us, Margherita," Salvatore called, tearing bread. She had filled her bowl and returned to the draining-board, eating there. He paused expectantly, then shrugged, mystified. "What is wrong with us suddenly?"

"It's the Englishwoman," Carlo said out of a crammed mouth.

Forrester wheeled on him. "Cut that out." Englishwoman was slang for whore.

"You know too much," Carlo retorted. "And you're too touchy."

"You wouldn't have the nerve to tell her to her face, so don't sneak it in behind her back. She thinks you're contemptible enough as it is."

Guiseppe chuckled sullenly. Carlo flushed and began: "If I spoke her language—"

"Stop it," Salvatore warned.

Luigi leaned forward, soup spilling from his spoon. "I speak English."

83

Surprised, Forrester looked across at him; Inger, too. "Is that so?"

"Not good, not bad, but I speak it."

"Then you tell the *signorina*," Forrester said in Italian. "Translate for your brother. Carlo doesn't care, so why should you?" He couldn't seem to let go. "Go on," he needled, but Luigi shifted awkwardly. "You're all the same. Salvatore's right. And she hates your guts—all of you."

Salvatore's eyes twinkled. "How d'you like our dynamiter, Margherita? *Simpatico*, eh? Not a vegetable." He blew hot and cold, now friendly, now threatening.

"What's Salvatore been selling you?" Forrester asked her. "That he can bring the walls tumbling down? Have you asked him how? He's trying to make the best of a bad job, but what's he going to do his magic with?"

"Don't listen to him, girl."

Across this Luigi was exposing more of his English. "You like the soup?"

Inger shook her head.

"What is wrong? Too much garlic, eh? The tourists do not like garlic—I know. I was a waiter once . . ."

To Forrester Salvatore growled: "We can get explosives—all we need. There are sulphur quarries within fifteen kilometres of here."

"You'll want more than blasting powder."

"We'll get whatever's necessary—don't you worry. Your job will be to tell us what's required."

"How the hell do I know what will be required?"

"That is for you to find out. And this you will do tomorrow. You will take the car to Monteliana and reconnoitre."

"Don't be ridiculous," Forrester said.

"Tomorrow," Salvatore nodded confidently, munching.

"You don't know what you're asking."

"I have a good idea."

84

"You can't have. I've never heard anything so—"

"Would you prefer to decide blind, then?" Impatiently: "All right—tell me here and now what you require and save yourself a journey. But be sure you're right."

"Look," Forrester argued. "You're asking for a demolition survey. What am I expected to do? Walk round the place openly taking measurements?—making calculations? Because that's what a survey entails. I thought you said this place is a jail?"

"A lock-up. You can see it from the hill."

"See it!"

"It is laid out like a map . . . a model. And you can drive past the main gate."

Derision seemed to tie Forrester's tongue. In the pause he heard Luigi ask Inger: "Do you know America? We have an aunt in America . . . Syracuse, New York." Siracusa, he called it.

"You can get very close to the main gate," Salvatore insisted. "And you can study the general lay-out from the hill."

"That won't be enough, I tell you."

"Then you will have to make some intelligent guesses."

Forrester stared at him. "This is lunacy. God Almighty, you keep talking about explosives and the main gate and the geography of the place as if they were the be-all and the end-all of everything. If you're hoping to take someone out of there you need a plan, a detailed workable plan, and I need to be told what it is. Otherwise you're heading for disaster."

"There'll be no mistakes this time—neither by us, nor by you." Salvatore's fists were clenched on the table. "You can't afford one, friend. In case you've forgotten let me remind you that it wouldn't pay you to fail us. You also have everything at stake."

"What is M.C.?" Luigi was asking.

Inger frowned.

"It is against his name. First his name, then M.C."

"I don't know."

"Is it a degree?"

"I can't tell you."

Forrester dragged his mind from his rearguard with Salvatore's unreasoning obsession. "Tell him what?" He'd heard, but it hadn't registered.

"I don't understand his question," Inger said.

Luigi asked him direct: "Is M.C. a degree?"

"No."

"What is it, then?"

Dismissively, without pride or interest, Forrester answered: "It's a Military Cross." And even as he spoke he remembered how his father had argued that it ought to be on his business card—"Dammit, Neal, why not? It's a *cachet* and—well—it can't fail to help once in a while. You know how I mean . . ."

"From the war?"

Forrester didn't reply. He'd never wanted it in print.

"How could you have been in the war? You—not forty yet."

"There have been other wars," Forrester said.

Salvatore touched his arm. "Luigi has fine English, eh? He will be company for the *signorina* tomorrow when you go to Monteliana. She won't feel so deaf and dumb with him around." His pale eyes reflected amusement of a sort. "You see, we have your welfare at heart."

"You're so bloody clever, aren't you?"

"More than you imagine, perhaps." Salvatore drew his free hand across his lips. "If things go against you in this country you become as clever as God allows and twice as desperate. They are a powerful combination, those two; they can remove mountains."

When he spoke in this fashion something ferocious showed

86

itself to Forrester. It bore the hallmark of a philosophy and way of life that had moulded everyone present except Inger and himself. Violence and revenge—with these and these alone could you survive or honour your obligations; without them you went to the wall or were disgraced. Corruption and deceit and indifference and death—these were the sum of Salvatore's hard cruel knowledge of the world and the people in it. And all this he inferred as he went on to speak about Angelo and the necessity of action: action was the first resort; there was no other recourse, no other law. All his years it had been so. Other things changed, oh yes—now droves of foreigners came, for instance, and stayed in hotels and swam in the sea and drank the wine; but what did they know of the realities? Nothing.

"Nothing," he repeated bitterly. "Like you."

Carlo waited a while, then said: "About the car—will it want the other number-plates? It's rented, don't forget."

"When is it due back?" Salvatore asked Forrester.

"Tomorrow."

"Better put them on."

"*D'accordo.*"

Forrester said uncertainly: "What's the idea?"

"A precaution—for you as well as for us. You will come back from Monteliana because of the *signorina*. Of your own free will. New number-plates are merely an insurance against outsiders interfering with your intention." Salvatore's chair screeched on the floor as he rose from the table. "We are perhaps not so foolish after all."

Forrester's tone was wooden. "If I'm going to Monteliana I have to know precisely what to look for." Incredibly, it had come to this.

"Concentrate on the main gate."

"Nothing else?"

"Nothing else." For the first time Salvatore spoke as if he

87

might admit to a plan of sorts. "And in case you should be confused by which gate is which, Margherita will ride with you in the car."

18

THE light was already losing its brilliance. Long shadows through the pines, a resurgence of bird-calls; dark would be swift.

There was no lavatory. Guiseppe moodily accompanied Forrester when he left the hut and Margherita went with Inger, stiffly, keeping her distance as if Inger carried a contagion. When it came to a wash Forrester walked to the falls and stripped and stood under them, the shock and force of the water only beginning to produce a glow by the time he returned inside. Behind the hut Carlo and Luigi were at work on the Fiat. Inger used the sink to wash in, the men withdrawing at Salvatore's insistence; it was bizarre politeness from one who threatened so much.

They had eaten for the last time that day. The sun set behind clouds, like veins in marble. As the light drained out of the air Margherita dragged the sacking over the windows and lit candles: inside, the place seemed to shrink and the world became more remote than ever.

Forrester retreated with Inger into the barred room, taking a candle with them. When he told her what was expected of him next morning she said: "Oh no!"

"I won't be away long."

"How long?"

"Perhaps a few hours."

The yellow glow emphasised the bone structure of her face; her eyes looked enormous, alarm dilating their physical beauty.

"Please don't go."

"I must."

"Not without me ... Please."

He took her hands. "They've got me on a string this way, don't you see? They know I'll come back."

"And you will?"

"Inger," Forrester chided gently. "Surely you don't think—?"

"I don't know what to think." A shiver racked her. "I'm frightened."

"Don't be."

"Half the time I don't know what is happening, and then when you explain things they seem to go from bad to worse. I keep telling myself it isn't true, none of it—these people, this ... this pigsty, what they want done. I can hardly believe we are part of it."

Forrester nodded. "But that won't make them vanish, it won't alter anything. They'll be here in the morning, and I'll have to leave you. Whatever they're cooking up is going to be as improvised when they get to it"—he had to clarify 'improvised' for her—"as it's vague at the moment. But they won't back out; they're not that kind. They're going to raid Monteliana for sure ... I'm not my own master, Inger."

The candle-flame leaned, then straightened, yet the air remained still. She released her hands from his and brushed her hair nervously towards her ears.

"Just as soon as I'm no further use to them they'll be finished with us," Forrester said.

"When will that be?"

"Two, three days." He paused, wondering: God alone

knew. "About tomorrow—with that young one, Luigi, you won't be as cut off as you might have been."

"Him!"

"At least you can communicate. That's better than nothing. If you want anything—"

"All I want is to go."

She sat motionless beside him. The blue trouser-suit belonged to promenades, cafés, sun-drenched streets—anywhere but here. The blonde hair, too. Earlier, from the window, Carlo had watched her returning to the hut through the trees and whistled. Now from the other room Forrester heard him say: "Has the Englishwoman gone to bed?" And someone—it might have been Guiseppe chuckled: "Where else do Englishwomen go?"

He gazed at Inger, empty within himself. At least, he thought, ignorance spared her some of the indignities. He moved round the bed, shook out the solitary blanket and spread it over the mattress. He took off his jacket and folded it into a pillow for her. Then he kicked off his shoes and lay down. Presently she followed suit. They lay side by side without speaking, weary from the rack of their minds. Beyond the door the voices rambled on, now sharp, now subdued, Salvatore's uppermost, in control. The room grew chilly, and there was dampness with it.

"Can I have the blanket over me?"

"Sure," Forrester said.

He got up, tugged it from under her and respread it. The candle had burned halfway down and he prepared to nip the wick.

"D'you want the light any more?"

"No." And then, in the darkness, she said: "I didn't know you had been a soldier."

"There's a lot you don't know."

"Were you?"

"Once. Of necessity."

90

Did it comfort her in some way? He didn't pursue the thought. Far off an owl hooted, lonely but free, and the falling water slopped endlessly on the boulders. The sound was like a drug, lulling Forrester towards sleep, yet sleep wouldn't come. Inger slept, though; suddenly, as a child might, curled up. Gradually the main room emptied. Forrester stretched out, sharing Inger's warmth. After a while he rolled gently off the bed and tried the door. It was locked and, as he eased himself beneath the blanket again, he realised he hadn't expected any different. Tomorrow was already a fact; tomorrow and whatever else was yet to come.

Sometime in the night Inger turned in her sleep and, sighing, put her arms round him. By then he was half asleep himself and he didn't stir; but he opened his eyes. And before he eventually went under he was asking himself whether he was being held out of habit or from fear. If it were fear then he also knew the need there was to be comforted, the hunger for it. He had always wanted affection, trust, to be liked and admired.

Mercifully there were no dreams.

19

IN the morning there was bread on the table and a pot of sharp black coffee on the stove. This was early, with the sun angled low through the trees and the air not yet warm.

Forrester shaved with his cordless razor, then walked over to the falls and rinsed his face in the icy water: no one followed—a mark of confidence in their hold on him. Nothing had changed. When he re-entered the hut he picked up the suitcases and took them into the room that had become for him and Inger a retreat as well as a prison. The contents of the cases were in disarray and he wondered who had pilfered what; his cash had gone, but at least his passport was there.

"What about yours?" he asked Inger.

She nodded, searching through a jumbled heap of clothing as if to distract herself with familiar things. He left her to it and went into the main room; the place was even more shabby in daylight. Guiseppe sat on the table smoking, one leg swinging, and his dead-looking eyes watched Forrester pour more coffee for himself. They were taking turns at ensuring that Forrester and Inger weren't outside together; three times now Forrester had passed Guiseppe sitting there and endured his surly stare.

With his back turned Forrester said: "I see you lifted my cigarettes."

"What of it?"

"I guessed you'd be the one."

Guiseppe stirred. "Are you getting at me?"

"You flatter yourself." He was inviting trouble, and knew it, yet the whispered warnings were ignored. "I couldn't be bothered."

Carlo sniggered, a release of nervous tension; Margherita, at the sink, stopped clattering some plates in the water. Guiseppe got off the table.

"I'll take what I like, when I like."

"I'm sure you will."

Forrester sipped from the chipped enamel mug, pettiness channelling the entire weight of all he felt so bitterly—humiliation, resentment, apprehension. He was hamstrung, reduced to sniping, yet the words came against his better judgment, with

92

a kind of self-daring. Guiseppe moved towards him down the room, provoked now, arms slightly bent.

"You want a cigarette?"

"Not from you."

"*Tanto meglio.* Because that's the only one you'll get"—and Guiseppe flicked the glowing stub past Forrester's face.

"Grow up, Guiseppe," Margherita snapped. "Haven't you caused trouble enough?"

"I don't like the way he talks."

"I don't like a lot of things, but I suffer them." She turned her back on him indignantly.

Carlo sniggered again. Forrester crossed to the window and stared out. He must keep a tighter hold on his tongue; Inger could suffer; a lout like Guiseppe believed in reprisals. Through the trees he could see Salvatore and Luigi returning from the falls, Salvatore rolling down his sleeves, Luigi finger-waving his hair as he walked. Little peacock. Salvatore pushed through the door, picking up a chunk of bread as he passed the table *en route* to the stove.

"Are you ready?" he asked and Forrester shrugged. "How about you, girl?"

"Whenever you say."

Salvatore placed an arm round her shoulders: there was affection in his hug, and the smile was genuine, even his pale eyes twinkling for a second. "You'll be in good hands," he told Forrester. "The best."

"I'll need to be."

"She knows Monteliana inside out." He bit off some bread. "*Mi ascolti.* You have got five hours. Five hours will be plenty. It is eight now. Monteliana is about forty kilometres, so you will be able to take your time there. But don't be late back." Until then his tone was almost conversational. "If you're even a minute overdue we will begin to think the worst—and that is the last thing you can wish to happen."

Forrester emptied his mug. He had no more cards to play; no fears to work on—except his own.

"It's the main gate—yes?"

"Correct."

"Is it to be demolished, or weakened, or what?"

"We'll think about that later."

"That's idiotic. I need—"

"Later."

"What if nothing can be done? Sometimes, for technical reasons—"

"If you come back and tell me a fairy story I won't believe you. I know that gate, friend. When will be the difficulty, not how." Salvatore switched cryptically to Margherita. "Have you got the letter?"

"Yes."

Forrester left them to collect his packet. Luigi was already at the door of their room offering Inger a tattered copy of *Oggi*. "There are pictures," he said. "No need to know Italian."

"I have to go now," Forrester told her.

The frightened look was there at once. "Promise you will come back."

"Of course."

"Promise." Her eyes searched his; from experience she would know where lies were hardest to hide. "Say you promise."

"I promise," Forrester said. "Truly . . . I'll be here before one o'clock."

He turned away. Guiseppe blew smoke as he passed. And to you, Forrester thought. To Salvatore he said: "I'll need some money—for petrol."

"Margherita has money."

"I also want your guarantee that Signorina Lindeman won't be molested in my absence."

"Don't you trust us?" Salvatore's expression was one of feigned injury.

"You, perhaps. I'm not so sure about the others."

"Haven't we struck a balance, you and I? After all, Margherita will be in your charge—isn't that sufficient guarantee?" He swallowed. "What do you want? A label pinned to her—*non toccare*, do not touch? . . . You worry too much, friend."

Forrester's mouth tightened. Margherita started for the door, working her arms into an old black cardigan, straightening the cheap gilt crucifix hanging from her neck. He followed grimly, and Salvatore came with them.

"Don't forget, *ragazza*—if we're not here, make for the other place."

It was the first time there had been even a hint that the hut wasn't secure. They had seemed so confident, keeping only a casual look-out, relying on instinct; yet this would be strong, animal-like. Now and again Forrester had seen them tense slightly, listening, then individually or collectively relax, something identified, dismissed.

The sound of the falls greeted them as they stepped outside and walked round to the rear. Forrester wouldn't have known the number-plate had been changed. He clambered into the Fiat; the engine retched and came reluctantly alive. Margherita opened the other door and got into the back.

"Five hours, remember," Salvatore said, cupping his hands.

Forrester released the brake. And as they drew away he saw Inger at one of the barred windows, watching them go.

95

H E threaded through the pines until he found the path and followed it to the track they had come along yesterday. Only yesterday? Time had lost its measure.

"Which way?" he asked curtly.

"Left."

North. They turned on the track and climbed out of the hollow. The awful barren vistas presented themselves again, silent and deserted under the bright sun. The hide-out was even more isolated than Forrester had imagined. Ahead, the skyline consisted of jagged, claret-coloured peaks. He kept the driving-window half closed against the dust and nursed the car over the gritty, pot-holed surface.

They must have covered a mile before either spoke again. Then Margherita said: "I must warn you—I have a gun."

Forrester glanced sharply at her reflection trembling in the mirror. "You won't need it. I've as good as got one at my head as it is." They juddered over some rock. He laughed bitterly. "And Salvatore talked of a balance. Some balance!" Then he said: "I'll bring you back, don't kid yourself. I've no option. Just tell me where to go."

She leaned forward. "I also have some cigarettes."

"No, thanks."

"My own. Not yours."

Forrester didn't reply.

"Not Guiseppe's either."

Something in her tone dragged a response from him. "All right."

"Here."

He reached over his shoulder and took one from a creased green pack; an Alpha.

"Have you a light?" she said.

"Thanks... For you?"

She shook her head. The track had made two or three more roller-coaster dips into wooded hollows; now it ran flat and almost straight, edging left, desolation to either side. Salvatore hadn't exaggerated: a battalion could search and never find them.

"Where were you yesterday?" Forrester asked; silence would make the journey even more intolerable.

"At the hut."

"You weren't there when we arrived."

"Oh—I went for food."

"Where, for God's sake?"

"To friends." None of them ever gave anything away—'friends', 'a letter', 'the other place'. They were professionals after a fashion, except in what they were about to attempt.

"On foot?"

"Of course. How else?"

She must have walked miles, he thought; and, despite himself, he marvelled. Saltpetre spat in the coarse tobacco as he drew on it. Some small birds scattered out of a clump of prickly pear as the Fiat lurched past. The track dog-legged between great outcrops of rock, pointing north-west. In the middle distance he suddenly saw a truck moving across their front and telegraph poles strung out like a line of stumpy matchsticks.

"Go left again when you reach the highway," Margherita told him.

For ten minutes after that they hardly spoke. When they got to the road and turned, the sun was behind them. Once there was a sign-post, but Forrester missed the name; and twice there were villages, each huddled about a church as if in self-defence against the wild, inhospitable surroundings, each squalid and soul-destroying, full of alleys and stained and peeling walls, dark doorways and alien smells and loungers who peered from angles of shade or ragged children who ran barefooted in brief pursuit of the car's dust.

Forrester said to Margherita: "Are you from that sort of village?" He didn't think of her by name.

"I am from the south," she said. "Chiara."

"Is it the same?"

"Is it poor, do you mean? Yes, it's poor. Nine-tenths of Sicily is poor."

Salvatore's scorn was in her voice, stressing the gulf between them; how could *he* know what life was like? He looked at her via the mirror: the careworn lines gave her face a handsomeness that she had earned, yet her eyes lacked all self-pity.

"Nine-tenths of Sicily isn't on the run."

"A man was killed. *Un vigile.*"

"So I gather."

"It was never intended."

"How long ago?"

"Five weeks."

"What happened? Did your husband—?"

Her interruption was fierce. "My husband killed nobody. *Nobody.*"

"Someone did."

"Guiseppe."

Guiseppe; that one. He might have guessed.

"It was never intended," she repeated. "They tried to break into the post-office at Caltanissetta but things went wrong. It was at night. Angelo was the only one to be caught. Last week he was sentenced to twenty years."

"Were you on the run before then?"

"Before, Angelo and I lived with his mother."

"Where?"

"Near Sommatina," she said guardedly.

"And the others?"

"Round and about."

"Salvatore, too?"

"Yes. Oh yes."

"What was your husband's work?"

"For a time he was in a canning factory."

"And then?"

"Then there was nothing. For a year there has been nothing. Guiseppe is a mechanic, though he could never keep a job, even when there was one. Carlo has done many things, but never for long. Luigi the same; he was always being paid off."

"And Salvatore?" Forrester swerved to avoid something squashed on the road.

"Salvatore is a carpenter. Or was." Angrily, as if she regretted having been drawn, Margherita said: "What does it matter? Can a man stop eating if there is no work? Does he allow his family to starve? He is driven to risk more and more —it happens everywhere, all the while, as God knows to His regret."

"Was the post-office the first time?"

"Together, yes."

"They never learn, do they?"

"What do you mean?"

"Now it's this—that's what I mean—trying to break your husband out of Monteliana on the strength of my knowing something about explosives. It's madness, sheer madness— surely you can see that?"

"Once he gets to Ucciardone prison we could never hope to touch him. It is like a fortress. Angelo has twenty years. Twenty—and for what?"

"A man died, didn't he?"

"Not because of Angelo."

"The law in my country would make him guilty."

99

Their voices were rising, one against the other. Her eyes flashed.

"Your country is no concern of mine. And the law isn't the same as justice. I can tell you what happened to—"

Forrester cut across her: "Where's the justice in what's happening to me and Signorina Lindeman? . . . Jesus Christ! Of all the stinking things." He moved a hand dismissively. "Please, not that."

"It is unfortunate."

"Thank you. Thank you very much. I'll remember that."

"Salvatore says—"

"Salvatore!"

Fingering her gilt crucifix she countered: "Salvatore is a good man."

"Oh sure. One of the best."

"You don't understand. How could you understand? You have never been under pressure before. You don't understand what it does to people, what it drives them to." In the mirror Forrester could see the moulding movements of her hands. "Listen—you will return to the hut; you said so yourself. And I know you will—even though I shall leave you for a while when we get to Monteliana. Why do I know? Because of that person. You could abandon her, yet you will not. You could inform the police, yet you dare not. So what will you do? Go back. She expects it of you, and you demand it of yourself. So it is with Angelo and me, and Salvatore and the others. We are under pressure, like you, but with us the pressure has been continuous and it began a long time ago." She tossed her head. "We are not what we are from choice. Salvatore is a good man, I tell you."

Forrester drew a deep breath.

"Look at the land here," she said. "What can it give? What hope is there? Even where it is better and there is work in the villages a man has the rich at his throat—the rich or the

100

mafiosi . . . If we were either of those would Angelo be where he is now?"

"The other question is, would the policeman be dead?"

She caught his reflected glance, but said nothing for a while. Presently, though, she leaned forward, pointing. "Left again at the turn beyond the windmill."

Twenty-two kilometres showed on the clock and three successive lefts had turned them roughly south. The sun streamed at them broadside on. Now they were running close under the lee of precipitous slopes with high serrated ridges and motionless cascades of loose stone overhanging the road. Imperceptibly, as the heat began to bounce, the eastward distances were shading to a hazy violet band that fused earth and sky. They passed another village perched on the brink of a ravine; farther on there were caves cut into the tilted strata of rock, some of them with crude doors and one with washing strung on a dead fig-tree jutting grotesquely above its entrance. The road twisted endlessly, the scene varying, yet its harshness growing monotonous. No coach-party ever came this way.

After a while they turned right, then left, then right again; Forrester lost count of the changes of direction. They were minor roads, not always metalled. He remembered a long, arched bridge across a river, a man walking with a coffin roped to a mule, one place-name that registered—Villalba, an entire complex of terraced cultivation that seemed to have failed and a vertically-corrugated hillside blanched white in the gulleys by a million years of sudden torrential downpours.

In silence Margherita watched the scene wheel and twist past. "They say God had lost interest by the time He was finished elsewhere."

Forrester drove on. Forty kilometres, Salvatore had said, so Monteliana couldn't be far now; his watch showed twelve minutes past nine.

"Say you brought this off, say you managed to get Angelo

101

out—what then? There will be a hue and cry. You can't hide for ever."

"We'll go away. Right away."

"Where to?"

"The mainland."

"That's easier said than done." Everything about this was easier said than done.

"Salvatore knows a man who will get us across."

She was holding to a dream and nothing Forrester might have said could have shaken it. Twenty years was a lifetime.

"Salvatore knew of the hut also. He has been in the hills before."

"Whose is it?"

Margherita raised her shoulders. "Who can say?" She stared in hatred at the desolation to either side. "People are leaving all the time, when they can. They pack and go—the mainland, America, Australia . . . They are the lucky ones, Holy Mary, yes. Anywhere is better than Sicily."

"These people left some things behind—table, chairs—"

"What are you thinking—that we stole them? What there is came from friends. We are not without friends," she said with pride. "Unless you have friends you might as well give up hope."

"What about guns?" Forrester flung at her. "What about hostages? What about applying pressure to someone else? . . . Don't you find them essential too?"

At nine twenty he saw a signpost to Monteliana; three kilometres. They were in a trough at the time, climbing fast. Sometimes the gradients were so steep that they seemed to be heading for the sky.

"A kilometre from here the road will divide," Margherita said. "You must take the upper road. The lower one leads into the town."

"And then?"

"I'll show you."

They made a couple of sweeping zigzag turns which brought them out of the trough. Now, suddenly, there was another of those startling drops to the left, birds circling below them. Just as suddenly, on the right, the hillside levelled off. The road-junction presented itself with Margherita saying, "*Destra, alla destra*," and they shied away from the brink and accelerated across a narrow plateau, waist-high with scrub and dotted with tamarisks. They passed a couple of hooded carts, their drivers asleep, and from one of them a child waved, cautious even in its innocence. For what could have been the thousandth time that day Forrester shifted through the gears. Perhaps half a mile blurred by, the road flanked by broken, dry-stone walls.

"This will do."

Forrester braked and turned off between a gap in the near-side wall, scrub and yellow flowering weeds brushing underneath the Fiat. He cut the engine and followed Margherita out, puzzled. There was nothing here except a worn stone plinth that bore the broken base of a statue and on which someone had placed a bundle of flowers.

"This way."

He went with her. They walked for about two hundred yards, Forrester trailing. The ground was uneven, and not until the last few strides did he realise they were approaching a cliff edge. Margherita stopped abruptly and crouched, beckoning him.

"There," she said, nodding as he came forward. "*Guardi laggiù*. Look down. That is Monteliana."

21

T HE view astonished him. The town was three or four
hundred feet below, filling a huge shelf on the hillside,
and beyond it, lower still, was the floor of a broad
valley, smudged and indistinct in the heat. Monteliana itself
seemed to vibrate in the glare. At first glance it looked for all
the world like a collection of toy bricks, saffron and white and
mauve, orderly at the centre, more and more confused towards
the perimeter, but all tight-packed and everything stunted by
the height and angle. Forrester could distinguish a square, a
tree-lined avenue from which narrow streets branched like
ribs, a blue-domed church, a severe four-storeyed building at
about ten o'clock which was enclosed and stood a little apart
from the town's limits.

Margherita noticed where his gaze was hesitating. "That's
the chest clinic. The lock-up is this way—right, well to the
right . . . Farther, here, here, almost beneath us."

Then Forrester saw it. For a moment it seemed so close that
he felt he could almost reach down and touch. Salvatore was
absolutely correct; the place was displayed like a model. He
was lying flat, propped on his elbows, and he moved slightly
forward, staring over for silent minutes on end.

The lock-up was well clear of the town, isolated on the
farthest extremity of level ground. The outer wall made an
exact square: it was difficult at such range to tell how high it
was, or how thick. Forrester's eyes followed it along—first the
side nearest him; there was a gate about a third of the distance
from the left-hand corner, a big, double-doored gate spanned
by a sandstone archway; the entire wall was of sandstone,
Forrester reckoned. This side faced north and the gate was

served by a road which led in from the town. The east wall also had a gate, about two-thirds along from the same corner, and like the other it was covered by an arch; an unmetalled track served this one separately. The south wall was unbroken, running close to where the hillside fell sheer away, but there was a small gate near the south-west corner of the west wall, narrow, wall-high but with no arch.

"Which is the main gate?" It wouldn't be the small one.

Margherita pointed. "There—the nearest to us."

Because of the arch Forrester could barely see it. He craned over a little more. The road linking with Monteliana went on past the gate and ended in a turning circle, presumably at some kind of view-point into the valley below; the tarmac was blackened with tyre streaks, but there were no cars in evidence. And there was no one about, which worried him: even a little activity would have been a comfort against his going down there and prowling around.

He'd brought a pencil and paper—it was the bill from the Capua—from the car's glove-pocket, and now he started on a rough sketch. He reserved judgment on the gate itself, doing his best to shut his mind to the criminality involved and the overall folly of the whole venture. There were five separate buildings within the lock-up's walls and he plotted them in outline, Margherita watching. They were all single storey, irregularly spaced, and gravel paths joined one to another across bare ground the colour of terracotta.

"What's the small building by the main gate?"

"Reception block."

"And the big one?" This was just left of the compound's centre.

"Detention block. There are thirty cells, plus the kitchens."

"How about bottom right?"

"That is the punishment block." Her tone was matter-of-fact. "Angelo's is the end window on the left."

105

Binoculars would have helped on the detail. A bulldozer was at work near by, levelling a mound close to the wall. There was no other sign of movement anywhere else within the lock-up.

Forrester switched diagonally across the compound. "By the south-east gate—what's that?"

"Offices. And the gate is the service gate." She knew the lay-out like the back of her hand.

"And over there—top right—is that a chapel?"

"Yes." It was screened from the rest of the compound by a low wall; some of the harshness was redeemed by a few flower-beds and a paved walk. "The small gate in the corner is for the priest and there is another—see?—in the inner wall."

They had kept their voices very low. Forrester shoved the sketch into his hip-pocket. Once before he'd stared down from a position as commanding as this, whispering with Singer as they contemplated his platoon's allotted front and discussed his chosen lines of fire. Nothing would ever be like that again for him, but he could feel the beat of his heart as he took a last long look at the lock-up. He was under the most elementary form of duress, yet it was totally compelling.

"That's all I want to see," he said to Margherita.

She nodded. They got to their feet and withdrew, crouching for the first few yards. As she got into the car she said: "Now we must go into the town. I will show you where to drop me. After that you must continue on to the turning-point alone. Salvatore said don't stop, whatever you do, or make more than one run."

"Salvatore," Forrester retorted in English, "can chase himself."

He reversed off the scrub and headed down the hill. When they reached the fork he swung right on to the town road.

"Is there no other way in and out?"

"No. It's a cul-de-sac."

They were into Monteliana after two or three tortuous

106

minutes. Suddenly, as the hill-shelf opened up, the town built itself around them; everything narrowed and buildings began to cut out the sun. Passers-by stepped on to sidewalks to let them jolt by on the cobbles and there were tight streets to either side with laundry strung from balconies—Forrester guessed they'd already entered the avenue he'd seen from the hill. The pale blue dome of the church was showing.

Margherita touched him on the shoulder. "Put me down here."

He braked obediently. She had a letter in her hand.

"Where do I pick you up?"

"Opposite. In fifteen minutes."

She got out and turned almost furtively, making a pretence of examining a shoe-mender's window. Forrester pulled away at once. Seconds later, in the mirror, he saw her detach herself from the window and hurry in the other direction.

Close to it was a tatty avenue, a seedy, sluggish town, coated with a bloom of dust, many of the houses windowless, Neapolitan *bassi*-style. The avenue ended at a T-junction and he made two random changes of direction, but it would have been hard to go wrong. The street he finally followed ran for about two hundred yards before open spaces began to appear, and once that happened the built-up outskirts quickly came to an end. First there was an untenanted stretch, then a waste-tip where men were forking rubbish, then another shortish gap of empty scrub and the lock-up beyond.

The road ran absolutely level and in line with the rock face from the rim of which they had looked down. Forrester slowed and opened both windows. He wished to God there was someone else in the vicinity. He was almost there now. A shallow ditch lay between road and wall, and the wall *was* sandstone, massive, about eighteen feet high. With a slight shock he then saw a uniformed man sitting on a chair in a bar of shade cast by the arch over the main gate—he hadn't spotted him from

107

above. The man yawned, eyeing him with boredom. With an effort Forrester lifted a hand in casual greeting, which was acknowledged. As he drew level the road split to turn across a culvert towards the gate. Iron-frame doors, wood planking, criss-crossed bands of studded iron strip, each door about eighteen feet high by ten wide—and already he was almost past. Two hinges on the pillars? He couldn't tell and he couldn't look back.

Christ, what a way to make a survey.

He held his near crawl, gazing about him as befitted a visitor's curiosity. At the turning circle he stopped and got out, stared blindly over the viewing balustrade with affected casualness. He could hear the snarl of the bulldozer inside the wall. After what he hoped seemed long enough for the man on the chair he went back to the car and started on the return. And then he had an immense stroke of luck. He was halfway to the gate when they began to be opened from the inside; the man on duty rose to his feet and helped swing the door outwards. A dark saloon was nosing through. Forrester slowed, ostensibly to let it precede him, but his eyes were elsewhere. *Three* hinges, bolted into recesses behind the sandstone pillars; he could see them perfectly. Strap hinges, the tapering straps reaching perhaps two feet across the wood. And the door was, say, five inches thick, eight to nine hundred pounds weight—guesswork again, but good enough, of no great importance.

- The saloon passed over the culvert and turned ahead of the Fiat with a gesture of acknowledgment from its driver. The temptation was to accelerate in its wake, but Forrester continued with the needle on the thirty-kilometre mark until he was past the waste-tip and the road had become an urban street again.

It could have been worse, a hell of a sight worse. And he'd got enough to go on.

. . . . . .

Margherita was waiting opposite the shoe-mender's. She was into the car without his bringing it to a standstill.

"All right?" she asked.

"All right."

"You have what you need?"

"I think so."

A few miles out of town he drew into the side and added some details on the reverse of the Capua's bill. "Never trust your memory"—Rice, the demolitions foreman at Peterborough, had this as his golden rule, and recalling it Forrester imagined his father's horror if he knew the purpose and circumstances of the sketch. But his father, Stone and Forrester, Peterborough—everyone and everything belonging to the normal pattern of his existence—were rooted in another world.

When he drove on again he was expecting more maze-like directions from Margherita, but she kept him to the main highway. It wasn't eleven when they left Monteliana, so there was ample time in hand. An occasional sign-post gave the distance to both Caltanissetta and Enna, and he realised they were completing a circle. There was other traffic for company, mainly trucks. Once, four *carabinieri* in an overtaking Alfa-Romeo ran level with them for several seconds, but Forrester's sense of isolation remained. He was a puppet; even in a crowd he would have been tied to Salvatore's strings. At Serradifalco he pulled into a filling-station and took on forty litres of petrol. Agip—so easily, at the outset, he could have said Agip instead of Esso. He resented having to ask Margherita for the money, his money, but indignities were something he was learning to swallow.

In a wayside village a little farther on she asked him to stop in the square, and she left him alone while she shopped in a fly-blown store. His money again. She came back laden and dumped the stuff in the car, then left him a second time to cross the square and enter the church. There were those, he supposed, who could kneel and pray that an enterprise would succeed, lighting a candle in token of their family's need or their own good name, believing as they did so that God, in His charity, would understand the dictates of their nature and the environment that had shaped and fired them. Margherita, evidently, was such a one.

A scabrous dog lifted a skinny leg against the car, children scrabbled languidly around a broken fountain, hollyhocks, self-sown in the angles of walls, wilted in the implacable heat. Forrester waited impatiently. He could never have conceived that he would be so eager to be with Inger again and hear that curious brittle voice of hers. For hours he had scarcely given her a direct thought, but now he grew restless. He was beginning to need her as much as she needed him.

By the time Margherita returned he had become angered by the extra delay, and it must have showed.

"Are prayers so wrong?" she said tartly.

He shrugged. "It depends on the prayer."

"Mine were for Angelo."

"Not even a candle for yourself?"

"I lit no candle."

"You should have done. You can afford it now—like the food back there. Or is theft too petty to worry about?"

"God forgives." The peasant face, the fanatical single-mindedness. "If you are sorry, God forgives. And I am sorry. I regret everything that has been done to you."

"Yet you continue with it."

"Because of Angelo. Because there is no other way."

"Even if it ends in murder?"

"I prayed for success."

"And if your prayers aren't answered—what then?"

"No one will be killed."

"Are you telling me that Salvatore's bluffing?"

She didn't answer. Even if she had said "Yes" he wouldn't

110

have believed her. A threat was measured more than by the form of words it took: what lit a man's eyes, what shaped his mouth—these were what chilled; and Salvatore's were unforgettable. There was no bluff. It was either, or—"as sure as God made Christ, friend . . ."

They passed through Caltanissetta well before noon. It was fierce country, less harsh than farther west, but Forrester wasn't sight-seeing. As they dipped then climbed away the landscape became more wooded and the views were stupendous, but he was virtually oblivious of them. Only when Etna's white cone briefly showed itself all of thirty miles away did it loose in him a pang of longing so strong that it bordered on grief.

Enna came and went, a mountain town that reared briefly around them. From there on he knew what he was looking for —the fork where Carlo and Guiseppe had trapped them. A different road, another day, another hour—so easily they might have been spared all this. Where, he wondered dully, were the Russells now?

"You turn left at the next junction," Margherita told him well in advance. "Sharp left."

"I know."

A few minutes later he made the turn, then took the track that led through the lawless wilderness to the hut. If he forgot anything, any single part of what had happened and what was still to come, he believed it would never be that first journey and the numbing moment Carlo had produced the gun. The whole nightmare had stemmed from there.

Stones crunched and spat beneath them as he drove in and out of three successive hollows. Then the dirt path was waiting for them, baked so hard that no tyre-tracks showed from his previous use of it; and the pines hid all trace of the hut's existence. The waterfall, too, was invisible.

111

Margherita stopped him when they were well short of both. She went forward alone until he lost sight of her in the trees, but she soon reappeared and signalled him on. He drove past her into the clearing and behind the hut, hating the sight of Salvatore as he came out and the sound of his deep voice as he greeted Margherita and the sight of the others and the sound of the water on the boulders as he cut the engine. Nothing had changed; nothing could change now.

Emerging stiffly from the car he saw Inger running towards him. "Thank God you've come back. . . . Oh, thank God." And, impulsively, his arms were round her.

"You're all right?"

"All right?—yes, yes." Half-laughing, half-crying. "I thought you would never get here."

"Has it seemed long?"

"A lifetime."

Forrester stepped back, sliding his hands from her shoulders to join hers. It was like a shot in the arm to his morale to see her relief.

"You shouldn't have worried. I promised, didn't I?"

Salvatore came stalking into view. "Welcome back, my friend. *Benvenuto.*" He was all smiles. "It was easy, eh? Nothing to it?"

"As far as it went. I could have done with more than a couple of passing glances."

"But you got what you went for?"

"I reckon so, yes."

Forrester walked with Inger to the hut; she still held him by the hand.

"You see?" Salvatore was saying alongside. "We kept our side of the bargain. She has come to no harm."

Guiseppe lolled in the doorway. "Bring the food in from the car," Salvatore ordered him. "Make yourself useful for a change"—and Guiseppe went, dead-pan, clipping Forrester's

112

shoulder with his as he passed. It was cooler inside the hut; the place seemed more cheerless, more resonant, than at any time before. In charcoal, someone had drawn a chequer-board on the table, and Luigi, who was cleaning a sawn-off shot-gun, explained: "I played with her." They had used coins as pieces. "She is good," Luigi said. "She won"—and he almost emulated Carlo's grin.

Forrester led Inger into their room, half-closing the door: privacy seemed the most natural thing in the world. There was a bond between them, compounded out of anxiety and mutual need. He could ignore Carlo's whistle which followed them in.

"It wasn't so bad then?"

"Now it isn't."

She smiled, standing close, her gaze very direct, and something moved in him. He kissed her on the forehead. The long fair hair, the soft colouring, the tanned skin—he had come to know them just as he had grown protective towards her and seen how indispensable he had become.

"I won't leave you again, Inger. In any case I think the worst is over as far as we're concerned. There's one more thing they want from me, and then—" He gestured. "From the way they've been talking they'll have finished with us very soon."

Salvatore elbowed the door open. "Very touching," he said, eyeing them. "But you went to Monteliana for a more important reason than this."

"All in good time." Forrester's retort came with a kind of bravado.

"Don't push your luck, friend . . . I'm waiting."

As Forrester entered the main room Margherita brushed by, laden up to her chin. Guiseppe followed, and Carlo and Luigi went after them hungrily—"Così va bene! . . . Un altro miracolo! . . ." Salvatore, on the other hand, didn't spare her so much as a glance.

"What about the gate?" he asked impatiently.

"There's no problem as far as I'm concerned."

"You are sure?"

"Quite sure. Given the right materials, that is. Technically, it's child's play. But you're going to have the devil's own job to get near it and place the charges."

"It will be at night."

"Even so."

Salvatore hooked his thumbs behind his belt. "That's a worry we can come to. Right now I want to know what the boys have to get from the sulphur quarries."

"I made some calculations." Forrester pulled back a chair and drew out the Capua bill. "Which way d'you want the thing to fall—inwards or outwards?"

"Outwards." From Salvatore's tone Forrester guessed he hadn't considered this before.

"How about blast? Blast's a factor if Angelo is going to be anywhere near." He paused. "Isn't it about time you told me how you hope to bring this off?"

"Later."

Stubborn bastard. Forrester opened the sketch map, ironing out the creases with his fingers. "Margherita says he's in the punishment block."

"Correct."

"How d'you get him out of his cell?"

"That will be arranged."

"Arranged?"

"Yes, arranged—for the precise moment."

"Is Angelo aware of this?"

"Not yet, but he will be."

"How, for God's sake?"

"You will hear later," Salvatore said tartly. "We have a saying—the less a man knows until he has to, the better his chances."

"And we have a saying—a little knowledge is a dangerous

thing. How far will Angelo be from the gates when you blow them?—I've got to know that when I make up the charges."

Salvatore raised his shoulders. "Thirty metres?" he conceded. He peered down at Forrester's rough outline. "What is needed from the quarries?—that is the important question. I want the boys moving soon. Make a list." He tore a page from the copy of *Oggi* where a boxed advertisement left white margins. "Write it there."

BUITONI PROTEIN BABY PASTA, the advertisement read, SPECIALLY PREPARED FOR CHILDREN. And Forrester wrote a child's list of explosives alongside. Ideally he would have requested a dynamo-type exploder, an ohmmeter, electric detonators, hand crimper—all these and more besides the basic requirement of blasting gelatine. But even if such items were available from quarry resources it would be asking far too much of amateurs to know how to handle them when the time came. The wisest course was to use manual ignition and rely on safety fuse, detonating fuse, plain detonators, and blasting gelatine cartridges. It was the most reliable way in the circumstances, provided the junctions were properly grafted and the charges correctly positioned. He could ensure the first by prefabricating the assembly himself; as to placing, this would need to be explained in detail and demonstrated on a mock-up.

Salvatore called Luigi away from the others and together they studied the list. Forrester added a few points of guidance for Luigi's benefit. Safety fuse was black, detonating fuse almost certainly orange, possibly orange-and-white striped; both came in coils and were likely to be packed in metal canisters. Non-electric detonators would be clearly marked as such, wax-paper wrapped in wooden boxes. The cartridges of blasting gelatine would also be boldly identified on the wrapper; plaster gelatine—in small slabs weighing about 100 grammes each—was an alternative.

115

"And if there are none of these?" Luigi frowned, his face clouding under the weight of so much information.

"Then Angelo stays where he is—it's as simple as that."

The wrong fuse, the wrong detonator, some crude primary blasting explosive—any or all of these would be equivalent to nothing at all.

"They'll get what's necessary," Salvatore said, adopting the bullying voice that he sometimes substituted for confidence. "They'll get it, you'll see."

Luigi returned to the list, studying the lengths and numbers of the separate items required. His finger-nails were as neat as a woman's.

"If you're in doubt bring more than I've indicated," Forrester said. "And, whatever you do, don't smoke—or rattle the detonators. Keep them apart from the rest, well apart."

"Carlo," Salvatore signalled vigorously. "*Venga presto a vedere*"—and Carlo came at once, munching an apple from Margherita's supplies.

He read the list quickly through, then nodded. "Okay. When do we start?"

For once his grin offended Salvatore. "Give your mind to it, boy," he growled. "We can't afford another of your mistakes. And be careful with the car; no madness with it."

"*D'accordo.*"

"*D'accordo,*" Salvatore mimicked. "I have heard that from you before . . . Now, are there any questions?"

Luigi shook his head.

"Carlo?"

"When do we eat?"

"Afterwards. *Christo!*" Salvatore eyed the bulge in Carlo's jacket where the pistol rested and saved himself a question. "Take your time, but not too much. We'll expect you when we see you."

They went then, Salvatore following them out. The keys

116

were in the car. *"Ciao, Margherita,"* Carlo called, and Luigi turned in the doorway, addressing Inger: "Good-bye, lady."

Forrester said to her: "From the way they set about it you'd think they were going shopping." He shook his head, amazed. There was an open pack of cigarettes on the table, his own brand, and he offered it before taking one himself. "They're getting careless—or generous."

"They let me have them while you were away."

He smiled. "It's easier for a woman—particularly a blonde."

Incredibly, something approaching jealousy touched him. He pulled a strand of hair away from her cheek and, sidelong, he saw Margherita swing her back on them in indignation. The car lurched past the windows with a parting bleep-bleep of the horn as Salvatore came up the outer steps.

"Wish them luck," he said.

"Isn't the place guarded?"

"An old man only. Today is Saturday."

"What will happen to him?"

"Nothing bad. Old men frighten easily."

"But he'll report the raid."

"Not until Monday morning. Until then, my friend, he'll be tied up in his store—safe and sound. He'll come to no harm. And on Monday, when they find him, he can report all he wishes. Angelo will be away then. It will be over. For you, too. You can go where you like, do what you like—as I've said, it won't matter to us. We'll have gone—won't we, *ragazza*?" he called along the room, and Margherita turned at the sink and looked her dream at him.

117

22

Tomorrow night, then. Salvatore was like a miser with what he divulged, but this was more than just another dark hint: Sunday night.

Forrester told Inger: "We'll be in Palermo by noon on Monday."

"Yes?" Her voice lifted eagerly.

"As sure as we're here now."

He took her outside. No one objected, but Guiseppe shouted at them to stay close and squatted in the doorway, cradling the shotgun, wearing a greasy cloth cap. Now and again he muttered threateningly.

"Do you remember what I said yesterday?"

"You said many things."

"Did I?"

"Yesterday was like a year."

"I said we'd laugh about this one of these fine days."

"Oh yes."

"Well, another forty-eight hours and we'll be able to."

"I will believe it when it happens."

"You'll be telling this tale to your kids and your grand-children—"

She shook her head. "When this is over I want only to forget. I shall tell no one. No one—ever. How could I? I do not tell people of my nightmares. And besides, it would cause trouble—for you most of all."

"I was only joking," he said.

They were sitting with their backs against one of the pines in front of the hut. Forrester spilled the pine-needles through his fingers. Very early on, when he had thought in terms of escape, of getting to a gun, say, of tricking one of them and breaking away with Inger in the car, it would have seemed impossible that the two of them could become an integral part of Salvatore's revised plan and that they should now wait helplessly for it to be put into action. For perhaps an hour at the beginning that desperate feeling had lasted—until Salvatore spelt out his terms. Even then, for a while, Forrester had hoped against hope for outside intervention, a fluke of some kind like a roaming police patrol chancing on the hut while they were together. But hopes like this were as wild as what Salvatore had in mind with all its risks and loose ends.

"Liar," Guiseppe railed suddenly. "You lied to me. And now we go to Monteliana. Because of you. Impostor!"

Forrester tried to ignore him, sorting his thoughts aloud to Inger above the splashing of the waterfall. They would need the car on Sunday night—that was obvious. Three of them, probably. Margherita and possibly Guiseppe would keep guard at the hut; one of the men, anyhow. The others would drive to Monteliana with the fuse assembly and the made-up charges. How they would effect Angelo's escape was still a mystery; there was more to springing a prisoner from Monteliana than blowing the main gate. But, assuming Angelo got clear, Forrester reckoned they would return to the hut, collect the other two, then vanish, make for the other place . . . And Monday would have come.

"You sound so sure," Inger said.

"I am," Forrester lied. The pine-needles spilled soundlessly. "We're only useful to them up to a point."

"Then I envy you." She would doubt more than most; nothing for her could ever have been certain. "Aren't you scared that something could still go wrong?"

"No," he said. But he was. Salvatore was unpredictable, the explosives Carlo and Luigi returned with might be totally

119

inadequate, Monteliana could be a disaster . . . They would be on the high-wire until the very end. And yet, to encourage her, he said: "No."

Inger lifted her head, staring up at the sunlight glittering amid the branches. "I said I want to forget all this. But, of course, it will be impossible to forget. Who could have thought, that morning when I called to you, that it would come to this?"

"I've been pretty useless."

"On the contrary."

Anger was natural to Forrester, but if he were honest with himself he knew that almost every futile act of defiance on his part had been because of her, the blustering and the verbal rebellion largely because of her, drawn out of him because her very defencelessness asked for some show of strength; it was expected of him for no other reason than that he was a man. Nolan, and whoever had preceded Nolan, and the others before that, all would have known this aspect of her; her kind of man provided, smoothed the way, made everything possible. And a man had to be dependant upon himself—which was something he had never been. The more he gave the more he needed support, the reward of flattery. It had always been so with him and now it was again. The future was something he couldn't contemplate with any assurance, but looking at Inger he felt the bond between them strengthen. The mobile eyes, the delicate neck, the long trousered legs, the pressure of her fingers on his—he told himself there might be joy between them yet. If . . . If . . . And again he began to fret inwardly about Monteliana and the razor's-edge that led to Monday and their freedom.

"How long were you a soldier?"

"Not a day more than necessary. National Service."

"Where?"

"In Korea."

120

"My brother was at Suez, with U.N.O. He is in the Norwegian army—permanently."

"Good luck to him. Soldiering suits some people."

"Not you?"

"No."

"Yet you were given a medal. Luigi said—"

"Oh that." Forrester shrugged. She had this image of him; Diana had had it, too. And for years he had conformed to it. "It was a hundred years ago, Inger."

"A hundred—"

"I was joking," he said a second time and smiled at her. Only once had he seen her laughing; it was at the casino, before the bottom fell out of her world, and he recalled how gaiety had transformed her. And could once more, given the chance. Yes, he thought. Yes . . . Then a bird skittered through the trees and he tensed fractionally; he had forgotten what it was like to be relaxed.

"Englishwoman," Guiseppe swore from the steps, self-goaded into another outburst.

"What is he saying?" Inger asked.

"He doesn't like us."

"He's the one who frightens me most."

"He's harmless enough so long as they need us. Anyhow, don't think about him. Concentrate on Monday." Forrester looked across at Guiseppe. "Why don't you shoot yourself?" he called in English. "*Figlio d'una putana.*" And felt Inger press against him.

Carlo and Luigi returned within two hours. The white car came flicking through the pines without warning and swung in a wide circle across the clearing before coming to rest behind the hut. Forrester rose to his feet simultaneously with Salvatore clattering down the steps.

121

"Yes?" Salvatore called as the car doors swung open. "Yes?"

"Nothing to it." This was Carlo, gesturing dismissively.

"What was on the list?"

"And more."

Salvatore wanted Luigi's confirmation. "All right?"

"I think so."

Carlo said: "We have enough to blow the sky away."

"It's what you got, not how much."

"It's all right, I think," Luigi said. "He had a small box of detonators in each hand. PALONI—Forrester didn't know the company; Paloni, Brindisi.

"No trouble with the old man?"

"No—though he had a dog. Carlo shot it." Luigi paused, half expecting abuse. "It would have barked night and day otherwise."

"Let's see what there is."

Forrester joined them at the boot. Carlo opened it with the flourish of someone who believed he had made amends, and they peered in. Safety-fuse, instantaneous fuse—several uncased coils of each caught Forrester's eye immediately; both were marked with hand-written stock-tags. Carlo lifted them out.

"This is how they were on the racks. It was easy. The old man checked the list for us. *And* wet his trousers." He laughed.

Underneath were three boxes, each with rope handles. A Paloni product again—plaster gelatine. It wasn't Forrester's first choice, but he reckoned it would do; a high velocity of detonation was required and the Nobel equivalent he was familiar with ensured this.

"What you wanted?" Salvatore asked sidelong. Forrester had never seen him so anxious as now. "You can manage with this?"

"I'd say so, yes."

Forrester lifted out one of the boxes: Carlo was right—they'd brought at least double the required quantity. He lugged the box into the hut and the rest followed, carrying the others. Within a few minutes everything was on the table.

"Tape?" Forrester queried, completing a mental check.

"Here," Luigi said, and dragged a roll from his hip-pocket. He also produced a few loose gun-cotton primers.

"Why those?"

"The watchman said we might need them."

"You mean you discussed it with him?" Salvatore flared. "You told him what this was for?"

"I said we were cutting metal."

"Ah," Salvatore grunted, relieved.

Carlo grinned his empty smile. "Do you think we are completely stupid?"

"Yes," Salvatore retorted harshly and raised a bent arm at him. "*Zitto!*" Then, to Forrester: "It is all yours, *amico*. Now you will want to make preparations, eh?"

"I can't do anything until I know what's in your mind."

Salvatore's face was like a poker-player's.

"When do you start for Monteliana?" Forrester tried.

"This time tomorrow."

"So I can complete the assembly in the morning?"

"If you wish."

"I won't be able to finish before the light goes."

"That's up to you."

Forrester waited. Salvatore might well withstand the lights and the rubber-hoses, but here and now his granite reluctance to give anything away was maddening.

"Don't you see that I can't make a start until I'm told how you want this done, where your people are going to be, what your timing is—?"

123

Salvatore moved his feet restlessly. "How much information d'you need?"

"The more the better."

"In the morning I shall tell you everything."

"I'm talking about now. Hell, if you expect—"

"No one is any the wiser yet. Not even the boys."

Forrester tossed his head. "You distrust them too—is that it?"

"No," Salvatore said sharply. "But for the present it is best that only one should know. Far better." He made expressive play with his hands. "It has always been so," he said, holding fast to some tribal rule, some code of conduct. "Always." He made no secret of it; all except Margherita were gathered round the table, apparently indifferent to ways and means, interested more in the lengths of fuse and the boxes of plaster gelatine, fingering them, muttering. Only Guiseppe scowled.

Forrester drew a long, slow breath. "All right. If that's the way it is then I'll tell you what I suggest is done."

"Very well."

"There are six hinges on the two gates. That means twelve separate explosive charges."

"Twelve?"

"Twelve, yes. I can put those together now. For the demolition to be effective they will have to be detonated at one and the same time. This is quite easily arranged by connecting each charge to a central stem of fuse and running it back to the ignition point. As far as I could see there are only two likely places for this to be—in the ditch between the road and the wall, or in the culvert under the approach to the gate itself."

"Which do you recommend?"

"One is as good as the other."

"What about the guard on the gate?"

124

In astonishment Forrester said: "D'you mean there's a guard?—at night?"

"Yes."

There was a pause. "Then you're sunk," Forrester said slowly. "You haven't a hope."

"He patrols. He circles the place every hour. For fifty minutes at a time the gate is unattended."

Forrester stared at Salvatore. A new hazard had been introduced; all the leads would have to be camouflaged, hidden— on the gate, across the ground. Placing the charges was enough responsibility for a novice without this. In any case, because of the guard the ditch was out of the question.

"It will have to be the culvert, then. But I don't envy the person who takes it on. He'll need four pairs of hands . . . Will it be you?"

"No," Salvatore said without hesitation.

"Who, then? He'll need to be shown how to set the charges on the hinges, he'll want to know about fuse speeds—"

"Tomorrow."

Forrester shrugged. The swarthy faces, the unimaginative minds; had they really grasped the extent of their unpreparedness? Rice, his demolitions foreman, would have wept. He picked up a spoon from the table and prised the lid off one of the boxes; the explosive was in rather smaller slabs than the Nobel variety, but well packed and waterproof-wrapped. He extracted one and peeled the double wrapping off, looking for signs of deterioration—sweating in particular. But there was none—a very slight natural glistening, but no more. The familiar pungent sickly smell seemed to cling to his nostrils; too long with it and invariably it gave him a headache.

"I'll have to test this," he told Salvatore. And when Salvatore frowned, he said: "I need to know its strength."

"You mean you will make an explosion?"

125

"It has to be done, otherwise I'll be working in the dark—more than I am already," he added tartly.

"How many explosions?"

"Two—perhaps three."

Salvatore was uneasy. "Couldn't this wait?" It was rare for him to be on the defensive. "That kind of noise carries. Why not do your testing tomorrow? We shall be quitting here then."

Forrester shook his head. "Until I know the quality and performance of the stuff I can't make a move. Take your choice. D'you want to bring this off or don't you?"

Salvatore pursed his lips, grunting while he considered. "All right then," he said at length. His eyes were full of suspicion. "But no tricks, mind."

"That's a laugh coming from you." Briefly Forrester's eyes found Inger's, instinctively looking for approval. Then he said: "I'll need a knife." Carlo shoved one of the table knives towards him, but he said: "Sharper than that. A razor-blade, if there is one."

There was a click and something flashed across him, thudding into the table-top only inches from his hands, quivering there; Guiseppe's knife. And Guiseppe smirked at him with surly venom.

"Sharp enough?"

126

23

FORRESTER cut a wrist-to-elbow length of safety-fuse— roughly twelve inches—then another piece three times as long. Every move he made was studied as if he were a street-corner magician. It was single core fuse with a black varnish finish, admirable for dry conditions. He took both lengths outside and lit them separately, close to the steps, timing them with the second hand of his watch. The first he clocked at thirty-one seconds, the longer at ninety-two, which gave him an approximate burning speed of two feet a minute— roughly what he had expected.

Satisfied, he walked around to the back of the hut where he'd noticed some scrap metal scattered amongst the kitchen rubbish. Salvatore followed him. Forrester kicked about in the weeds and pine-needles—a rusted petrol can, some wire, a holed bucket; none of it was of any use. Then he stumbled over a piece of iron bar; from the look of it he guessed it was a spare from the bars used on the bedroom window. Half-inch by three-inch, about four feet long. He carried it back into the hut and set about making up a simple test charge.

The plaster gelatine was in 100-gramme slabs. Four, there-fore—if his rapid conversion was correct—would give him as near to a pound as made no odds. He took two of them out of the box, peeled off the wrappers and loosely taped them to-gether; except for the clinging smell it was like handling gritty brown Plasticine. Again, every move he made was watched in silence. Then he cut a twelve-inch length of safety-fuse and six feet of instantaneous, cutting them square across the stem. The knife-edge was razor-sharp. He worked steadily, without hesi-tation, sure of himself. ("You're wasted behind that desk of yours," Rice had once told him. "You ought to be showing the apprentices how it really should be done.") But long ago that, long ago. His fingers lacked practice.

Now and again he spoke, explaining like an instructor to raw recruits. "This explosive is fairly pliable, as you see . . ." One of them had to know. "Instantaneous fuse is what the name implies; it detones at around 6,000 metres a second . . . The explosive and the fuses are perfectly safe to handle; naked detonators, though, must be treated with respect . . ."

The aluminium detonators were in cardboard tubes, upright in their box. Forrester tipped one out, fitted it over an end of the striped instantaneous fuse and crimped the neck carefully with his teeth. (No apprentice would have been encouraged to do that.) He capped the safety-fuse with a second detonator, which he then taped along the instantaneous near its open end, leaving an inch or so overlap. "Bring the bar," he said to no one in particular, picked up the fuse assembly and the double slab of explosive and turned to go outside. As he left the table he saw Carlo raising a cigarette to his lips.

"Jesus Christ!" He knocked it flying. "Don't you ever listen?"

Carlo flushed angrily. "It wasn't alight."

"*Sciocchezze!* Any moment and it would have have been." Forrester glared, no bravado now. "Take chances with this stuff and you pay for it—haven't you got that yet?"

He walked outside, shaken. They'd never bring it off; they weren't disciplined enough: fearlessness and lack of imagination were no substitute. He went over to the waterfall, the others trailing, Luigi carrying the iron bar. Salvatore covered Forrester with the shotgun, as if to prevent the explosive somehow being turned into a weapon against them.

"No tricks," he warned again. "Don't be clever."

"If you use that thing it will be your funeral, too."

Forrester took the bar from Luigi and wedged it horizontally between two of the mossy boulders. Then he opened up the slabs of explosive, about to sandwich the end detonator half-way in.

"Get clear now."

As everyone withdrew he inserted the detonator and moulded the explosive carefully round it, then taped the charge tight to the upper side of the bar about one-third along its length. Going back to the others he said: "Now I'll have a cigarette."

Luigi gave him one, flicking a brass lighter under his nose. Forrester walked forward again, bent down, blew on the cigarette tip and applied it to the safety-fuse. As it caught and began its slow, spitting run he turned and retreated, not hurry-ing, thirty seconds in hand.

Without tamping, two hundred grammes might prove a shade too little; there were so many factors. He halted beside Guiseppe and waited, sheltered by the boulders, and as usual the final seconds dragged until the detonation cracked like a giant whip. Dust erupted in an inverted cone as the air shook concussively, fraying the cord of falling water, raining needles out of the nearest pines. In the momentary quiet that followed Forrester seemed to hear the echo chasing away into the dis-tances. With his ears singing he rounded the boulders and re-turned to where he had jammed the bar. It had ruptured straight across, absolutely clean. He picked the two pieces up, more than satisfied.

"Good, eh?" Salvatore said, visibly impressed. There were fan-like scorch marks on one of the boulders and the enclosed space had an acrid stench.

Forrester nodded thoughtfully.

"So you need experiment no more."

"Once more."

"No."

"It's essential. I can't base everything on—"

"The risk is too great. That noise—" Salvatore tossed up his hands.

"Better to risk something now than have a total failure at Monteliana."

"If you hope to bring the *carabinieri* running, *amico*—"

"If there were hopes of doing that don't you think I would have used a kilo of the stuff instead of two hundred grammes? You'd have been none the wiser until it was too late. They would have heard it in Leonforte."

"What you used was loud enough."

"Listen," Forrester said wearily. "I'm sick to death of this. You broke my back yesterday, but you also gave me your word. Okay—and you've got mine. To the best of my ability I'll see that you go to Monteliana properly equipped, and I'll explain and demonstrate precisely what has to be done so far as the gates are concerned. But I can't do it your way. I'm going to make one more test. If your threat to Signorina Lindeman and me means anything at all I'm not chancing my arm by gambling on what I'm responsible for. And I wish to God I had as much confidence in the ability of the rest of you."

He turned past Salvatore and started towards the hut. "You're a strange man," Salvatore called after him. "You believe me, yet you doubt me."

"Right," Forrester flung across the clearing.

"It's as well that you believe me. And tomorrow you will have no doubts. Tomorrow you will know how well I have planned. Everyone will know."

"Everyone except Angelo."

"He already knows all he needs."

"Since when?"

"That letter Margherita took to Monteliana was for the priest."

"And the priest is your ally, I suppose?"

"Without being aware of it, yes."

Inger was sitting on the steps. She smiled uncertainly as Forrester approached and accompanied him into the hut. He had a sudden desire to hold her and to be held, made to feel indispensable. For a moment just now as he confronted Salvatore he had felt terribly alone; the single-handed strain of coping with the demands upon him and shielding Inger from the secret extent of his fears was beginning to undermine his will. They weren't out of the wood yet; the worst could still happen. Deep down the uncertainty ached like a cancer, and there was a longing in him to be strengthened, comforted by one who felt for him, needed him and could make him better at doing what he was being forced to do.

All this he felt as he came into the hut with Inger and went to where the explosives were boxed on the table. Margherita was at the stove, cooking, and she glanced round to see who had entered, conveying her hostility to Inger with her eyes; they were savage whenever she looked at her, critical and contemptuous, and Forrester reckoned it fortunate that language separated them.

"How long will you need the table?" she asked him.

"Ten minutes."

"The meal is ready."

As if to spite her Forrester put an arm round Inger's shoulders. "Hungry?"

"Yes."

"I won't be long," he said to her.

He opened the box of plaster gelatine and this time took out three slabs, slicing one of them in half with the knife. Then he cut the same length of safety-fuse as before and capped it with a detonator, binding this to two lengths of instantaneous placed side by side. Each he capped in turn with a detonator.

Salvatore and the others had come in and stood watching;

131

and again he explained in simple terms what he thought they should know—that the delay between initiation and explosion could be controlled to within a few seconds by the amount of safety-fuse employed, that the instantaneous fuse and detonators together triggered the explosion, and that—unlike the first test—he wanted to see whether the bar could be sheared by cutting from both sides with smaller individual charges.

"By the time I've put twelve charges on to the final fuse assembly it will be a pretty heavy and unwieldy load—and the uppermost hinges on the gates are about four metres off the ground, remember. The more weight I can save you, the better."

They traipsed out after him. He jammed what remained of the iron bar across a crevice between two boulders, inserted the detonators, then taped the charges against the bar, one on top, one underneath, allowing a half-inch gap between them. As he bound the tape he said: "The way you do this is vital. The explosive must be in perfect contact with the metal—see? And by leaving a gap between the two charges you produce a shearing effect . . . Right, give me a lighter, someone, and get clear."

He waited until they withdrew, lit the fuse, then joined them. The detonation was a shade more powerful than the first; the air seemed to go grey around the stabbing core of flame and the waterfall flattened sideways into the bluff as the blast sucked back and forth. A mist of spray momentarily covered them.

Salvatore screwed his eyes, face lifted a little as if he were following the sound-wave beyond the hollow, trying to gauge its range. Some birds wheeled high overhead, screaming. Forrester led the group back behind the boulders and again there was the acrid smell that plucked at memories in him. The bar had severed, less cleanly, but completely satisfactorily.

Guiseppe picked up the shorter piece, then flung it down

132

with a yelp as the heat of the jagged end burned his hand. Carlo laughed. *"Che spaventapasseri!"* He would have laughed, Forrester reckoned, when he shot the dog at the quarry. Sympathy was as alien to him as a foreign tongue.

"Satisfied?" Salvatore asked Forrester gruffly.

Forrester examined the quality of the break and nodded. Yes, as far as circumstances allowed, he was satisfied. The bar approximated in thickness to the hinges.

"Good, then we can eat." As they crossed the clearing Salvatore seemed to find it necessary to bait him, as if he sensed that his authority had been diminished by allowing the second explosion. "You are worried, aren't you? Inside. Why? I wonder. Are the boys worried? No—yet they are no better informed about Sunday night than you. They have faith, that is why. Faith in me."

"Guiseppe, too?"

"Of course." Salvatore stopped in mid-stride. With scorn he said: "You are a foreigner. How can you understand? What a man does at the time is the important thing, and on Sunday night everyone will play his part. Wait and see." He started to walk again. "These games with dynamite, a few grammes more or less . . . It was unnecessary. You can be too clever, too cautious. Caution drains the guts out of a man. When we raided the post office at Caltanissetta we—"

"When you raided the post office at Caltanissetta you made a hash of it, and listening to you I'm not surprised. You're all piss and wind, and it scares me more than—"

Salvatore grabbed Forrester by the arm, swinging him round. "Listen, you." The colourless stare was bright with rage and his voice shook. "If I didn't need you I would kill you now. Mother of God, I would!"

24

THEY sat in the same places at the table, the tension electric, Salvatore scowling as he wolfed his food, the others silent, uneasy. And Forrester thought: What gets into me? Where's the sense in provoking him? . . . He'd been more angry than afraid until now, but his skin had crawled as Salvatore released his grip. It was as if he were extending himself beyond the point where anger and resentment and uncertainty were prepared to go: something other than these kept prodding and demanding. He shook his head slightly as he ate the stodgy *lasagna* Margherita had prepared. It was no time for self-analysis. He felt tired, wrung out.

Again Margherita chose not to sit at the table, and no one pressed her. Besides the pasta there was cheese and fruit and a different red wine, less thin but coarser. Everyone ate hungrily, Inger included, but the brittle silence continued. Now and then Forrester would glance up to be met by Guiseppe's brooding stare or find himself intercepting Carlo's avid study of Inger. The fat police officer in Taormina had hardly been more blatant, but Carlo's interest combined an element of awe with the youthful lust; blondes swept past in cars, sunned themselves beside pools, danced in the cool of the night where the bands played and the money was. He would have seen them, glimpsed them—and whether beautiful or not they would have been different, remote, unattainable. Always unattainable, even now, though never in such prolonged proximity or in so unprivileged a situation. It seemed natural to Forrester that Carlo should feed his eyes and mind on her, yet a part of him objected, objected but did nothing; from now on, as best he could, he was going to curb his tongue.

Carlo was the first to finish eating. "Get outside," Salvatore ordered him, mouth full of bread. "Keep a watch on the track."

With reluctance, Carlo started to go. "For how long?"

"Until someone takes over, that's how long."

The explosions had unsettled Salvatore. His rage with Forrester wasn't long sustained but his continued anxiety was clear to see. Twice during the meal he rose and peered out at the clearing and beyond. As they broke up after eating he told Guiseppe and Luigi to share hourly stints with Carlo, then he cleared one end of the table and, with a knob of charcoal, began to draw an outline of Monteliana.

The boxes had been stacked in a corner. Forrester took the long coils of instantaneous fuse into the open and set about the laborious task of making up the basic assembly, using his own rough sketch of the lock-up for reference. Inger came and squatted beside him as he sat with splayed legs and began cutting the fuse into lengths.

"I wish I could help," she said.

"Just having you here helps. You've no idea."

"Is this dangerous, what you are doing?"

"Not dangerous, but it's vital not to miscalculate or to make a bad junction."

"Junction?"

"Join."

He started to explain, but soon realised she wasn't really interested: being with him was what seemed to matter, sharing the silences with him as he worked, and he was grateful.

Already the light was on the ebb. He had allowed for an ample amount of fuse in his calculations, and Carlo and Luigi had brought more than he'd listed, so there was no risk of being short. But, inevitably, all his measurements were approximations—the gates, he reckoned, were pivoted about seven yards apart, the pairs of hinges set at roughly three, seven and a half

135

and twelve feet off the ground, the distance between the gates and the culvert at least eighteen yards, possibly twenty, and the culvert the same width as the gates, better say eight yards, nine to be on the safe side. In every case he over-estimated. It wasn't a complicated assembly but it called for great care. By the time he had finished the central stem of instantaneous fuse would quickly split into two and the separate branches would then sprout double leads to each of the hinges: but there was no hope of finishing there and then.

The sun was beginning to leave a red smear in the west when he quit and went inside. Margherita had lit candles and was fixing the sacking over the windows. At one end of the table Guiseppe played cards with himself; at the other Salvatore studied his outline of the lock-up and the buildings within its walls, his tattooed hands flat on either side, fingers tapping.

"All piss and wind, eh?" he growled as Forrester passed. "Tomorrow you will eat your words."

Forrester said nothing. He carried the loops of fuse into the small room, then returned for the boxes of explosives. Carlo was leaning against the sink, playing a harmonica; Luigi had gone on watch.

"In the morning you will be surprised," Salvatore persisted. "We have a saying—'No Admittance' and 'No Exit' mean nothing to a fox. Angelo will have seen the last of Monteliana by dawn on Monday—always provided your dynamite does what it should."

"It will."

"Make sure of that." His eyes renewed the threat. "Make very sure, friend."

25

INGER had taken a candle into their room. Forrester went in after her and shut the door. He sat on the side of the bed and began making up the twelve plaster gelatine charges, using one and a half slabs for each. Candlelight was good enough for this, but not for grafting fuse. Inger was lying down; the damp chill was rising again and soon she pulled the blanket across her legs.

"When will you be finished?"

"Not long."

She looked at him. "You're tired, aren't you?"

"A bit," he nodded.

Beyond the door someone laughed; Guiseppe? And the sound of the harmonica came close, very close, wheezing out a saccharine melody; then Carlo sniggered and moved away, his juvenile charade over.

"That one is a child," Inger said tartly.

"With a gun."

She reflected for a while. "Do they say things about us?"

"Sometimes," Forrester admitted.

He finished loosely taping the charges and stacked them away; then he stretched out beside her.

"What is the time?"

"Quarter to seven."

"I have never been to bed so early," she sighed. "Never since I was little."

No? he thought. And then he wondered whether Nolan had been buried yet, claimed yet: at least his ghost seemed to have been laid.

Outside the window the pines stood motionless in the

strengthening starlight. One of the men left the hut and presently one came back—Luigi, relieved of his stint; his accent was less marked than any of the others. A chair scraped, a bottle clinked against glass, footsteps sounded about the room and the various voices mingled, clashed, bridged the silences on their own. Carlo must have gone out again; there was no harmonica now. Forrester brooded, following them about in his thoughts. Once he heard Salvatore say: "Come and sit, *ragazza*. Come and take some wine. You have worked enough, and tomorrow night you will need your strength. The last hours are always the longest"—and as usual there was that rare affection in his tone, a genuine concern, as if he knew from the past what it was to have been softened by a woman.

Forrester slid his feet under the blanket, not tired so much as weakened by everything the last two days had done to him. He lay with his hands behind his head, gazing at the mildewed ceiling in the dim yellow glow of the single candle, deliberately distracting himself from the pathways in the shadows of his mind.

"Can you see South America up there?"

"South America?"

"On the ceiling—that shape." He pointed. "Don't you think so?"

"I can't see South America."

"You're looking at the wrong thing . . . What else can you see?"

"A horse, perhaps," Inger said after a while.

"Where?"

"In the centre of the patch of light. Upside down . . . A small green horse."

Forrester searched the area in vain. "Your imagination must be better than mine."

How often had he played this kind of game?—counting the

138

paces between lamp-posts as a boy in order to forget the dark, willing on himself a good exam result if the traffic-signals were green three times in a row. Everyone played it in one form or another, killing time, side-stepping issues. Singer had done so one night in Korea as they waited for the moon to rise, playing his own version of it then, drugging himself with talk about apple-blossom in the Kentish Weald when the spring came, and some pub or other, and the feel of a pewter tankard, and how May was often the best month of all . . .

"The other day," Inger changed tack, "you said you had been married."

"That's right."

"Were you divorced?"

"No."

"Is your wife dead?"

"She died in a car crash."

"I am sorry."

"Seven years ago. We were in Portugal." For some reason Forrester felt impelled to go on; even this was a distraction. "There was no other car—it wasn't that sort of accident. Diana was driving and she misjudged her speed as we came into a corner. She braked and we skidded through the posts and over the top. Both of us were flung out as the car somersaulted. About fifty feet from the road the hillside plunged straight down—a sheer drop. The car disappeared after the first bounce and I thought Diana had gone with it for a moment—until she called, that is. All I could see were her head and arms; she was literally clinging to the edge of the cliff. I started down and got very near . . . very near. But there was a lot of loose stone and the edge kept crumbling away . . . Our fingers must have been within a foot of touching." He broke off for a few seconds, then added: "She was an excellent driver normally."

"I am sorry," Inger repeated. "You need not have told me. I didn't mean to—"

139

"It's all right."

He wasn't one of those who found it easy to unburden himself, to expose the secret places, the lost hopes, the shattered dreams. Only twice in his life had he been overwhelmed by the need to speak of what was buried in him, and both times he had just arrived home—once from Korea and once from Portugal, once to an enthusiastic welcome, once to shocked commiserations. Home was the place where you went and they took you in; yet it was also where what he had tried to squeeze out of himself never came when it mattered. Inside he'd been crying for help—both times, desperate to let someone share every numbing gun-flash cameo of that rearguard action, or how Diana's eyes had stared at him when her grip started to go and the slithering sound of the sliding shale as it swept her away, or Corporal Dunbar's scream "My legs, sir! Jesus, my legs!" as the blood pumped on to the mud from the jagged stumps of his thighs. All that and more, more. Sharing it would have helped, but each attempt had been a failure. Instead there was his father at the party and the embarrassing little speech, champagne in hand; his father on the telephone, ringing his cronies. ("Yes, Neal's home. In very good shape, thanks, none the worse for wear from the look of him"), his father alone with him and saying: "The M.C.'s a damned fine decoration. Well done, Neal. I'm proud of you." No help there, no ability to pierce the stiff-lipped barriers between them, neither then nor after Portugal and Diana's funeral, walking together between the pruned roses, their collars turned against the wind—"You did everything a man could, Neal. My God, you almost went, too. Now you've got to be practical and think of the future, only the future. There's no other way, believe me . . ."

Kindness, yes; sympathy, yes; generosity, yes. But something lacking, the failure as much his as anyone's. So there was no bitterness, no sense of grievance. Only a layering over, a moving on. And now there were check-points where memory pulled up short, as if to spare him from himself.

"Are there children?" Inger asked.

"Children?—no."

"Brothers? Sisters?"

He rolled his head. "We're a very small family. Aunts, uncles, cousins—I could count them all on one hand."

"Is your mother dead, too?"

"Oh yes." A portrait above the fireplace. "When I was three."

Salvatore coughed at the table. There were fewer of them with him now; two, at least, had gone to the other rooms, and no one went on watch after Carlo. "Bring him in," Salvatore had muttered around nine o'clock and Luigi had said, "He'll be glad. It's cold out there." Was Salvatore still poring over that charcoal sketch? Surely he had made his mind up by this time? . . . Some minutes earlier Forrester had heard a scratching sound at the door and guessed that they were being locked in. He accepted it without bothering to make sure; there were no options open to him, and never really had been.

"What kind of place is Peterborough?"

Inger's face was profiled by the candle-glow. He said lightly: "Do you honestly want to know, or are you just filling in time?"

"Both."

"Oslo is an alternative."

"If you like. Have you been to Oslo?"

"Not yet."

She looked at him. "Either is better than dirty spots on the ceiling."

"I can only speak for Peterborough."

She smiled, turning, and the straw mattress crackled softly. With one hand she pulled the blanket up to her shoulders.

"When was your plane—today?"

"This morning."

"So you would have arrived by this time?"

"Easily. Peterborough isn't exactly out in the wilds."

"D'you live in a house?"

"A service flat . . . And you? You'd have been in Oslo if your Consul—"

"I suppose so."

"It'll be Tuesday or Wednesday now."

"Monday is as far as I'm able to go. Monday and Palermo. You still believe it, don't you?"

"Certainly."

Salvatore belched and shoved away his chair. The sliver of light under the door angled and vanished as he passed along the room. He must have been alone, for as soon as he went the soft splashing of the waterfall and the silence of the night filled the hut.

"Nothing's changed," Forrester said to Inger, like someone reading a part. "It's all over bar the shouting."

She reached out and touched his face, as if in gratitude. And all at once desire flooded him. And suddenly he was lost in the sensation of his mouth and body against hers, clumsily, painfully; it had been a long time. For a few seconds a wordless passion possessed them; then she pushed him away, partially releasing herself to twist round and extinguish the candle on the floor beside the bed. The dark swallowed them and the room vanished.

"Neal," she whispered. "Neal."

The skill of her lips and, fumbling, the coolness of her breasts.

"When—?" she began.

"Don't say anything."

Being wanted and wanting in return. Like this, and like this. A glimmer of starlight touched her spread hair and hinted at the structure of her face. She giggled like a guilty child

142

when the rusty bedsprings creaked. And when the frenzy came
a tiny corner of Forrester's mind was prepared to stifle her cry.
But there was only the smallest whimper from her. Presently
she curled away, and he lay on his back, the blood-red darkness
beating behind his closed eyes, his brain wonderfully at a
standstill.

"Inger?"

Half asleep: "Yes?"

"Nothing."

26

H E was the first to go outside next morning. Pinned to
their door was a scrap of paper on which was scrawled
in capitals *NON DISTURBARE*. Angrily he tore it
away. Margherita, the only one there, eyed him covertly from
beside the stove.

"Very funny."

"I am not responsible. I do not make that kind of joke."

"I forgot—you just hate people, isn't that it?"

Watch yourself, Forrester thought. You don't want another
day like yesterday.

When he came back from the falls she had the coffee on the
table. The sketch of Monteliana was smudged by the passage
of hands and the movement of elbows, but remained perfectly
distinct. Forrester studied it; a few arrows pointed cryptically,
and clear of the north wall Salvatore had placed a cross and

ringed it round, but a worthwhile interpretation was impossible.

"So eager, friend? You surprise me." Forrester looked up; Salvatore had emerged from the end room, buckling his belt. "How are the explosives?"

"They'll be ready."

"When?"

"In good time."

"We leave here late afternoon."

"I'll have them for you by noon. And this afternoon I can give detailed instruction to whichever one you nominate."

Forrester re-joined Inger. She was only just waking. He kicked the door to behind him. "Hallo," he said quietly. Nothing, he felt, could ever be quite the same again.

She blinked at him. Dishevelment suited her. "Is it late?"

"Eight-ish. And only twenty-four hours to go."

He ruffled her hair, then rounded the bed and shaved. It was strange, but for a few moments he could hardly remember a time without her. She pushed herself off the bed and he watched her admiringly, very conscious of her now as she thrust her head and arms into the white sweater, watching with a fresh awareness that seemed like maturity.

"You're beautiful. Did I tell you that?"

Everyone was drinking coffee in the big room—Salvatore, Carlo, Luigi, Guiseppe, Margherita; all of them were there, and they were impatient, uneasy, without even an aside between them as Forrester emerged. Salvatore downed the last of his coffee and began darkening the lines of the sketch with a new piece of charcoal, whistling tunelessly between his teeth. He continued like this for several minutes, sometimes glancing at one or the other almost as if he were deliberately provoking an opening question.

Eventually he succeeded; from the window Guiseppe grumbled rebelliously: "When are we to be let into the secret?"

"I am ready when you are."

"*Madre!* I have been ready for two days."

"For two days you were ready to intercept the Russells, but the waiting addled your wits."

Guiseppe raised his eyes to the ceiling. "Who goes? What do we do?"

"Sit down," Salvatore said. "Sit down and listen—all of you . . . You too, Margherita. Each of you has a part to play. Listen as you have never listened before. And remember—"

"Who remains here?" Guiseppe again.

"Do you hope it will be you?"

"Why should—?"

"Monteliana will be no place for boys."

Guiseppe flushed. "I wouldn't take that from anyone else."

"Calm yourself," Salvatore said easily. "Calm yourself and listen. Luigi stays. Luigi is the youngest."

"That is unfair," Luigi protested, hands spreading.

"You stay, and that is final."

Standing by the wall, Forrester was relieved: anyone but Guiseppe.

Salvatore bent his shoulders over the outline on the table. "Everything will depend on timing—so I begin with the timing. At dusk we leave and travel by the back roads. We need to be given an estimate of how long it will take to fix the explosives" —this with a gesture towards Forrester—"but that is a separate matter and we can return to it later. By five in the morning all must be ready—and this is why. At five, the priest will be roused at his house; at half past, entrance will be made through the side gate." He indicated the small gate in the south-west corner of the west wall. "At quarter to six Angelo will confess through the speaking-hole in his cell door."

"Ayee," Carlo broke in uneasily, quick-witted for once. "Where is this leading?"

"Instead of the priest at the door it will be one of us. Angelo will confess nothing, but he will learn everything." Salvatore stared at them, the pale eyes bloodshot. There was a long pause. "Are you suddenly saints? Are you all so pure?"

Guiseppe licked his lips. "I don't like it."

"You I expect not to like anything," Salvatore flared. "But listen, all of you—how else can we warn him? You know about the letter Margherita delivered."

"Not what was in it."

"It was asking the priest to say a Mass for your mother on the anniversary of her death, and for Angelo to be—"

"Monday is not the anniversary."

"*Esatto!* You know it and Angelo knows it. Wasn't she his mother, too? . . . Put yourself in his place. He has been waiting for something from us—a sign, a hint. We promised him, remember?" Salvatore paused, looking across at Margherita. More gently, he said: "Does it offend you, *ragazza?*" And when she refrained from raising her eyes to him he began tapping his chest with both hands. "If there is a sin it will be mine, and mine alone. I am dealing with the priest, I shall be wearing his clothes. He comes and goes without restraint and so shall I. It is still dark at that hour. The morning Mass is at a quarter to seven, but there will be no Mass. Other things will have happened before Angelo is escorted to the chapel." He paused. "Very well. If this offends you so forget that you ever heard it from me. Shut your ears and pretend what you like, but Angelo has to be contacted." Then, exasperated by their silence, he flung at them all: "Now I see how wise I was to keep everything to myself. You would have fretted and argued your guts away."

Luigi remaining at the hut, Forrester thought anxiously, Salvatore entering past the chapel . . .

"All right, all right," Guiseppe said sullenly. "Go on."

"Now we come to the bulldozer. That surprises you, eh?

146

The driver enters the service gate a little before seven, but to-morrow morning we will be inside before him."

" 'We'?" Carlo asked, nibbling at his knuckles.

"Guiseppe."

Guiseppe stiffened slightly. "How?"

"You will come through the priest's gate with me and wait in the chapel enclosure." Salvatore pin-pointed the place with a blackened finger-nail. "At six-thirty you climb the enclosure wall and start the bulldozer."

"And—" Guiseppe prompted.

"You don't like it, do you? Your face is as good as a second tongue."

Guiseppe, Luigi, Salvatore . . . That meant Carlo would place and detonate the charges: not an encouraging choice.

"You're the mechanic," Salvatore said. "That is why I chose you for this. You are the one to get the bulldozer working."

"And if I can't?"

"Then we fail, just as we fail if I cannot get to Angelo or if we cannot blow the main gate. If we think about failure we will end with failure. So listen. There is a towing-chain on that bulldozer—you have seen it when looking into Monteliana from the cliff. You will hook it to the bars of Angelo's cell and rip them out. I have watched grilles removed during clearance work in Agrigento and they come away like dead wood from a tree."

"Grilles, maybe."

"These bars will be no different. Within two minutes of starting the bulldozer Angelo will be out of his cell. You will have at least that amount of time before anyone raises the alarm; you are hidden from the reception block and the inner guard on the main gate and no one will immediately question the bulldozer going into action half an hour early."

This had all the makings of a shambles, one gamble

147

precariously balancing another: it was a house-of-cards of a plan.

"Then?" Guiseppe said, scowling at the lay-out.

"Then Angelo rides with you across here." Salvatore traced a confident line from the punishment block. "When you are halfway to the gates the dynamite will be set off and you can crash through what remains of them."

"The wall at Monteliana is as high as three men," Carlo protested. "If I am to blow the gates, how will I know exactly where the bulldozer is?"

"That will not concern you."

"But it will, it must."

Salvatore shook his head. Straightening, he said: "You will be on top of the cliff. The sun will have risen and you will flash a hand-mirror when the bulldozer is halfway to the gates. That is your job, Carlo, that and no more." He looked at Forrester. "Our friend will be outside the walls, waiting for your signal."

And Forrester, rooted where he stood, stared back like someone betrayed, alarm clenching in his stomach.

"You are the expert, you see," he heard Salvatore saying. "The specialist. We are all incompetents, not to be relied upon—you have made that very plain. I am being wise and acting on your advice."

Forrester's voice shook. "I gave you no advice."

"It was implied. You stressed the difficulties, the technicalities."

"I can still teach someone precisely what to do. In an hour. In detail. The assembly will have been made ready, everything prepared."

"We have risks enough without taking on another."

"I am a risk." Desperately Forrester stepped forward. "You've gone back on your word."

"No."

"You said you would have no interest in us after a certain stage."

"After dawn tomorrow. There is a price for your freedom."

"I've paid enough." He could feel their eyes on him. *"Ho pagato abbastanza."* With the rage of the deceived he bawled at Salvatore: "I won't do more."

"But you will. I have already warned you of the consequences."

"Warn away—and be damned. Two can play at this game."

He turned, unaware that Inger had come out of their room, cannoning into her. He caught her by the elbow, meaning to retreat with her, lock themselves in, find safety of a sort—God knows. His mind was spinning. "What's happening?" she began, startled. Guiseppe blocked the way, his flick-knife like an extension of his right hand.

"Mi lasci passare," Forrester gritted.

Without warning Salvatore gripped him from behind, one arm round his throat; he must have moved like a cat. Inger let out a cry as Forrester was snatched from her.

"There are more than two. That is your misfortune, *amico* . . . Now"—to Guiseppe—"take her outside."

"No!" Forrester shouted.

"Outside," Salvatore commanded. "Who cares?"

Guiseppe prodded the knife into the small of Inger's back.

"Neal. Oh God, Neal"—she was wide-eyed as she passed Forrester.

"Stop it!" he appealed to Salvatore. "Call him off. Call him off, d'you hear?"

"Only if you change your mind."

"Yes. Yes."

"You understand now?" The grip was released. "How many times do I have to tell you this is not a game?"

Coughing, Forrester leaned against the wall. Through

149

watering eyes he saw Inger come like a blur across the room and he took her in his arms as if she belonged to him.

"You understand now?" Salvatore repeated.

Breathing hard, Forrester said: "See if you can persuade the *signorina* that you aren't a murdering, blackmailing bastard."

"*Zitto!*"

"Let him have it," Guiseppe snarled.

"We need him, fool!"

"Again and again he scores off you."

"But who wins, eh? Who wins when it counts?"

No one was moving. Forrester said bitterly to Margherita: "Is this what you lit your candles for?" Then to Inger. "It's all right. It won't happen again. I'm going to do as they say."

"Do what?" She was trembling.

"Blow the gates for them." He wasn't able to decipher what was in her look. Relief, was it? Nothing more? A part of him wanted more. "At first I refused. It was never part of the deal. They lied to me."

Or had he deceived himself? There and then he couldn't make sense of his thoughts. All he knew for sure was that he would never forget this place, this lousy room, the dark cynical faces of these people and what they had brought him to: and he feared what he might be brought to yet.

27

SHATTERED, he listened to Salvatore go over the plan a second time.

Leave at dusk; reach Monteliana before eight. Drop Salvatore, Carlo and Guiseppe off at the fork before the town. Drive on through and reverse the car under the lee of the refuse tip, close in by the cliff. No lights after clearing the outskirts. All night in which to place the charges—almost nine hours . . . At five Salvatore knocks up the priest. At half past he and Guiseppe enter by the chapel gate. At a quarter to six contact is made with Angelo. At six thirty Guiseppe climbs the inner wall and starts the bulldozer, hooks the towing-chain to the cell bars and rips them out. Then the crucial signal from Carlo on the cliff-top and the detonation and the rush to the car . . .

It was no less crude on second hearing, no less hazardous. Forrester gazed at the outline of the lock-up in a state of dismay. Technical know-how was not enough. In his mind's eye he could picture the gates, and the culvert, and the distance between, and the patrolling guard. He was going to be dangerously exposed, in need of all the luck there was; and if luck ran out for any single one of them it would run out for him too. All he could visualize was disaster.

"Afterwards," he asked Salvatore woodenly, "where do I pick you up?"

"At the fork again—Carlo and me. Guiseppe and Angelo come through the gate, you and Margherita—"

Forrester echoed her name in astonishment.

"You said the dynamite would need two pairs of hands. She will be your other pair." Salvatore measured him with his bloodshot stare. "It is her wish. She won't fail you if that is what you're thinking. She is not that kind."

Twice more they covered the details, leaning over the table, pointing, gesticulating, arguing nervously. Only Margherita took no part. And Forrester soon left them; he knew enough. With a kind of heartbreak he went into the small room and set to work on finishing the fuse assembly.

"The girl's coming with us," he told Inger. "But it could have been worse for you."

"Who will be here?"

Even now he could sometimes forget how isolated she was. "Luigi. At least he's got a little English." Dapper, pigeon-toed Luigi, almost a boy still, the least dangerous of them all. "It won't be so bad."

The fuses were already cut to length. Forrester began fitting the detonators to the branch leads. Somehow nothing seemed quite real again. He was years removed from the sharp end of danger, unpractised, unprepared. In a way that he couldn't explain he wanted Inger to fear for him, and as he bound the first leads to the main stem of instantaneous he wondered whether she really understood the situation. He had buoyed her up so often that he must have become infected by his own deliberate optimism, and now, when with hindsight he could see the inevitability of Salvatore's use of him, he asked not for tears or drama from her but at least some show of concern. She seemed withdrawn, calmer again but remote, very quiet as she watched him, as if she couldn't yet grapple with the turn of events. And he wondered for a moment whether she had watched Nolan spin himself to ruin with the same lack of awareness. Yet she had been warm and fierce and generous when she gave herself; did she know no other way?

"I never thought," she said, "it would be as easy as you made out."

152

"There was always a chance."

It was in his nature to judge people by what he needed from them. And what he believed he needed now was something to shield him from his own uncertainty. Pride forbade him from showing it; the confident front remained inescapable.

"It goes on and on," Inger said, the curious accent suggesting blame. "And every time they ask more."

Forrester's retort was sharper than he realised. "They're warped and bitter and empty-handed, but they've got what they want out of us now." He'd said this before, he knew.

"If the raid fails? They told you if the raid failed—"

"It won't fail."

"How do you know?" Nerves made her toss her hair.

"You mustn't talk that way." Viciously he snapped off some binding-tape. "I'll be here by nine tomorrow morning. Somehow I'll make it."

Yesterday, he thought suddenly, you said: "Promise. Promise." And yesterday had only involved an arm's-length reconnaisance. Now he searched her face for a glimpse of what he was after and decided that he saw it—deep in the clear eyes, like a foretaste of pain, loss.

"What you hope for is one thing," she faltered, "but what may happen—"

"What I hope for is time in Palermo with you when tonight is over. More than anything I want that." Forrester paused. "Don't you, Inger?"

"You wouldn't be interested in me afterwards."

"You're wrong," he said. "You don't know how wrong you are."

He bent over the snaking assembly of fuses, trying to give all of his mind to it. The world beyond here was a different place; he could cope with its demands; nothing there would be as extreme as this. But he could see a continuing need for her when they were safe again and his present strained version of

153

himself could be shed like a second skin. A longing like an ache mingled with the raw, prickling anxiety over what lay between and had to be accomplished first. It was the need to be strengthened, awakened again.

28

H E had the assembly finished by eleven. For once Margherita was not at the stove or the sink; she was sitting on the steps, darning the hem of her skirt.

Forrester went to her and said: "Unless you intend to be a passenger tonight there are one or two things you'd better learn."

He was curt, and her mouth tightened angrily. *"Quando?"*

"Now."

She followed him in and watched while he roughed out a diagram on the table of the main gate and the culvert. In the simplest possible terms he then explained what had to be done, drawing in the instantaneous fuse branches that would lead to each of the six hinges. They fanned left and right in pairs, the second pair longer than the first and the third longer again in order to reach the higher hinges: the overall assembly had the look of a squid-like body with enormous tendrils reaching out from its head, and each tendril then split to form a kind of claw. When they got to Monteliana, Forrester told her, he would tip each of these ends with a detonator and one prefabricated charge; then, too, he would tape to the base of the central stem the short ten-second piece of safety-fuse and the initiating detonators. Not before, not with the kind of roads they'd meet on the way.

"You needn't concern yourself with this," he said, "but it will take time, perhaps half an hour. I'll need you from then on, though."

"I'm listening."

"Salvatore says the guard circles every hour."

"The one outside, yes."

Alarmed, he said: "Is there another?"

"Inside the wall."

"Where?"

"He patrols, like the other one. We have not been able to check his movements, but he comes and goes from the reception block."

Close to the gates: Forrester ran a hand over his mouth. How much more would he learn?—and perhaps too late?

"Are you certain about the outside guard?"

"Quite certain. We have watched him from the cliff. On several nights. He is away from the gates for about fifty minutes at a time."

"When did you watch?" Forrester asked suspiciously. "I thought the original idea was to buy Angelo out of there, to bribe someone. Nobody's watched since I've been here."

"Before then. Two or three weeks ago. To begin with Salvatore had decided on a raid, but the more he considered it—"

She shrugged and Forrester finished for her. "The more impossible he realised it was."

"It is not impossible now. Not with the dynamite. And with you."

He bit off the retort that sprang to his tongue. "Look," he said, indicating the diagram. "The fuses will lead out of the culvert, on either side, and stretch across the ground to the bottom of the gates. They've got to be buried, covered over, otherwise the guard will see them. They needn't go deep—a

155

couple of centimetres will do—but it means we'll have to score the ground flanking the surfaced drive-in." It was baked weed-sown earth as he remembered it, iron-hard probably. "There's a tyre-lever in the boot of the car; we'll see if it's any use in a moment. If not, we'll find something that is . . . Now tonight, covering the fuse is a job you can put your hands to. If you're correct about the guard we'll have three-quarters of an hour or so."

"I am correct," Margherita said stubbornly.

"The next problem will be the upper hinges. They're too high to reach unless I climb to them, but I doubt if there are any easy footholds." He'd thought of getting to them by inserting himself between the pivot-end of the gate and the recessed angle of wall, forcing himself up like a rock-climber in a chimney with knees and shoulders wedging him in position. But with help there was a better way, quicker and quieter. "So for the top hinge in each gate you can stand on my shoulders."

"And place the dynamite?"

"I'll show you how. It isn't difficult. You'll never take my weight."

Carlo had come to listen. "Mind how he holds your legs," he grinned at Margherita.

"*Lasciami sola!* Go away and practise with your bit of glass."

"Phweee," Carlo said, raising his hands as if to ward off a blow. "You should hear yourself—dynamiter."

He was tense despite the show of teeth; they all were, keeping clear of each other—Guiseppe cleaning the shot-gun at the other end of the room, Salvatore somewhere outside, Luigi at the door where Inger was. "You want to play chequers, *signorina*? Pass the time? I will beat you today, you see . . . No? . . . Sure?" The sense of unreality swept Forrester again, and with it there was something like a momentary touch of fear, a tightening in the belly and the thighs.

156

"Come," he said to Margherita. "I'll show you how to lay a charge."

He took a couple of slabs of plaster gelatine and some spare lengths of fuse; tape was in his pocket. As he led Margherita to the car Salvatore called from across the clearing.

"What are you doing?"

Forrester ignored him.

Salvatore shouted: "I don't want any more of that." He loped towards them, light on his feet. He had been shaving at the waterfall. "No more explosions."

"I'm not exploding anything."

Forrester opened the boot and took out the tyre-lever. The ground scored easily, but it was soft and yielding. He walked a little way to where it was trodden down around the steps into the hut; considerably more pressure was required, but he could scratch out the sort of shallow trench that would be needed without too much difficulty.

"You try," he said to Margherita.

"What is this?" Salvatore grunted.

"We'll have to sink the fuses."

"Ah."

"That's about deep enough," Forrester said. He bent down and laid a short length of fuse in the depression. "Then we cover it over and tread the earth flat—gently though, very gently. The fuse will take your weight and more, plenty more, so long as you don't apply it violently . . . All right?"

"*D'accordo.*"

He pulled up the fuse and went back to the car with her, Salvatore on his heels like a second shadow; he would doubt him to the last, Forrester knew: trust was an accolade, hard won, rarely given. Forrester squatted beside the rear bumper, motioning to Margherita.

"When you place the explosive against the hinge, lay it flat, then tape it firmly—so—making sure you have absolute

157

contact." He ran the tape twice round the bumper, and when he looked at her enquiringly she nodded. "There are two charges for each hinge. Place the first on the side nearest to you, the second on the other side, but not quite opposite each other." He demonstrated. "Not like that, but like this—with a few centimetres between the opposite ends. Got it?" She nodded again, very grave, very intense. "As far as I could make out the hinges project about twenty centimetres from their mounting in the walls . . . Now you try."

He took off the tape and handed her the two slabs. She was quick, her fingers extremely deft.

"Didn't I tell you?" Salvatore said admiringly. "I've given you the right assistant, eh?" He stroked the nape of Margherita's neck. "*Che ragazza!*"

The afternoon seemed never-ending. Forrester was as edgy as the rest of them. For a time he went outside with Inger, partly to escape Carlo's incessant harmonica-playing, partly to seek refuge from himself. From the steps, Guiseppe warned them to go no farther and Forrester obeyed without any answering taunt. He stood with Inger in the splintered light beneath the pines and made a final effort to ease her mind.

"Whatever you do, don't panic when we've gone. Don't try and make a break during the night or anything like that. Luigi will be as anxious as you are by morning. And if the worst comes to the worst and there's a delay as far as getting back here's concerned—*if*, I said," Forrester stressed, "he'll be the one who's ready to clear off. He'll have their alternative rendezvous, wherever that is. He won't hang on indefinitely."

"But—?"

"Wait for me. I'll make it even if the others don't." How he hid himself away.

She lifted her face, the gaze direct. "Neal," she said, then hesitated.

158

"What?"

"A week ago you would have passed me in the street."

"So?"

"Don't expect too much. Trouble comes of expecting too much. You hardly know me."

"I want to."

"Yes," she nodded. "But—well, you owe me nothing—remember that."

"Inger, Inger."

He thought he understood; nothing had lasted for her, the future had never been measurable in more than a few days. In her eyes was the look of living with an absence of discovery. And he could change that—if his luck held until morning.

29

A T five, Salvatore called everyone together and held what passed for a final briefing session. And as if to reassure himself that there was no misunderstanding about the time-table he concentrated on question and answer.

"Carlo—where will you be?"

"On the cliff."

"When do you give the signal?"

"When the bulldozer is half-way between the punishment block and the gates."

"Have you got the mirror?"

"Here, yes."

"Good . . . Now you, Guiseppe. What time do you climb the inner wall from the chapel enclosure?"

Forrester didn't wait for them to finish. He started loading the explosives into the car. Very carefully he coiled the fuse assembly and wrapped it in a blanket which he obtained from Margherita. The gelatine slabs he packed into their original rope-handled box; unarmed they were harmless enough no matter how much jolting they received. Spare detonators and a fresh roll of tape he carried on his person. The wrapped assembly fitted comfortably into the boot and he persuaded Margherita to let him have another blanket to cushion it still further; the box of explosives he loaded separately, wedging it on the floor in front of the driving-seat.

It was soon done. When he went back in, Margherita was clearing the table for a meal. They ate soup again, soup and bread and cheese, and they ate in silence, the decisions come to, nothing left to dispute, everything agreed. The dusk was thickening, but they sat there in the gloom. Only when they had finished did Margherita drag the sacking across the windows. Then, in the candle-glow, Salvatore turned to Carlo: "Give your pistol to Guiseppe."

"But I have the shot-gun," Guiseppe said.

"Leave it with Luigi. He needs something here. You and I travel light."

He rose, his intention plain. Time to be leaving; time to go. There was activity suddenly, as if a spell had been broken. Salvatore bent close to the solitary candle, loading a heavy revolver; to Forrester it looked like the old British Army break-back, but he gave it only a passing glance.

"Good-bye, then," he said to Inger.

"Is it now?"

He nodded. "Keep your fingers crossed. Wish me luck."

He couldn't bring himself to say more. There was a feeling like lead in his heart. His smile, he knew, was a failure. He squeezed her on both arms, then turned away, and as he walked to the door he remembered he had first seen that lost

look on her face when Nolan had abandoned her and left her
to fend for herself.

He clattered down the sagging steps into the dark blue of the
evening. Luigi followed them out, nervous, trying to joke.
Salvatore got in beside Forrester; Carlo, Guiseppe and
Margherita into the rear. The doors slammed. Forrester
switched the headlights on and fired the engine.

"*Ciao*," Luigi was calling, tapping the glass. "Safe and
sound." Then Carlo, winding the window down: "Look after
the Englishwoman."

Forrester turned furiously in his seat. "Listen, you—"

"Let's be moving," Salvatore grunted impatiently.

"Tell Angelo I wanted to be there."

"Yes, yes."

"*Ciao*, Margherita."

Forrester turned the Fiat in the clearing, the tyres not grip-
ping well in the yielding ground, pine-needles spitting out
behind them. The door of the hut was shut as they rocked
slowly by, and Forrester threaded through the trees, dismayed
for Inger as never before and filled with a sense of deprivation
that seemed to choke his mind.

30

THERE would be no moon, only the stars. Twenty past
six and they were pricking through. The box pressed
against Forrester's calf-muscles, but it didn't hamper
him.

"Left," Guiseppe ordered as they neared the track. "*Alla sinistra.*"

The roundabout way. Forrester relied on the sidelights once he had straightened up and was pointing north. The landscape was even more forbidding in the silvered darkness, even more lonely. When they eventually struck the highway that lay across their front Forrester made his turn without prompting. He drove with dipped beams again, not fast, taking no risks, and two or three times they were overtaken, once by a low-slung Lancia that snorted past and away.

"*Prego,*" Carlo called derisively.

The villages Forrester remembered: they loomed up out of the night and trapped them for a while in their narrow slots of streets. Figures silhouetted in lighted doorways, a few shadowy people on the pavements, singly or in pairs, and the same hot ancient smells that seemed to reek of decay. On the outskirts of the second village Salvatore asked him: "You want petrol?"

"No."

"There's a filling station ahead. There won't be another."

"We're okay," Forrester said.

It came and went almost immediately. Forrester accelerated by, shifting through the gears. It was imagination, he knew, but the places he recalled seemed farther apart from each other than under the sun; he was looking for the windmill minutes before it showed. If he had been alone he would have sworn that he had lost his way, but Salvatore had no such qualms. Insects kept pinging against the windscreen and Forrester had to put the wipers on to clear the glass. Eighteen kilometres on the clock.

"Shouldn't we be turning left?" In the same breath he saw the windmill rising against the star-scatter so there was no need for Salvatore's "Yes, now—a hundred metres."

Then the dog-legging began, the endless changes of direction

162

through the wilderness. For perhaps twenty minutes almost the only words spoken came from Salvatore—*"Alla destra . . . Alla sinistra . . . Dritto, dritto."* He sat forward, hunched, watching the road as it bucked and twisted into the swinging beam of the headlights. The hills reared up and fell sheer away; the warm night air came licking in through the vents. Once in a while a yellow glimmer identified a solitary shack or a cave where life went on. Was that 'other place' a cave? Forrester asked himself: more than likely. But he had had his fill of wondering about them. They were silent in the back; he could feel their tension and it heightened his own. In under an hour they would reach Monteliana, and then the madness would really begin. Already he was sweating very slightly.

A T-junction lay ahead; vaguely he recalled it. He swung right on to a metalled surface, and all at once his heart missed a beat. A truck was askew across the road, half in the ditch, and someone flashed a torch at them in warning.

"Carabinieri," Salvatore hissed.

A gasp from Margherita. Forrester hesitated.

"Keep moving!"

Forrester cut the headlights and nosed forward. The torch kept flashing at them.

"It's a breakdown."

"Merda!"—Guiseppe.

Half-blinded, Forrester shielded his eyes. All this in moments. They drew level with the *carabinieri*, who stepped aside, waving them on. He bent forward, looking in at them as they went past. Then they were clear, drawing away, and everyone started jabbering at once, gesticulating with relief. All except Forrester; he hadn't these safety-valves; but the sweat seemed to chill on his skin as his pulse thudded.

"You should have blessed him, Salvatore," Carlo laughed, high-pitched. "You are the priest."

And Salvatore erupted: "Enough of that!"

163

Forrester glanced at him hurriedly, seeing him in profile—
the hooked nose, the crinkled hair. There were other fears, sins
as well as crimes. But to each his own. Forrester drove on. An
animal's eyes glowed in the headlights and he dabbed the
brake; God, he was jumpy. How far now? He remembered the
bridge, high like an aqueduct; remembered Margherita saying: "We are not what we are from choice. We have to make
this raid and it must succeed . . . *Must*." And he thought:
Must—yes. He saw himself lying dead, or a fugitive, or a
prisoner, the headlines, the scandal: Neal Forrester, Peterborough, company director . . . Until now he'd been an acces-
sory. But no longer. And no longer was there any appalled
confusion. Of necessity he had become one of them, wanting
what they wanted, even though he hated them for it.

A few kilometres more showed on the clock. His eyes and
arms ached from the concentration. Seven twenty-five. A car
passed in the other direction, one of the few they'd met. Forrester's mind drifted to Inger for a second; so much he had left
unsaid. Their whole time together had been strained, furtive,
unreal in a way. He'd misled her and misled himself; with any
sense he might have seen what was coming—though what
difference did it make now? All that mattered was getting
back to the hut; tonight meant a kind of revenge for the
others, but there would be no revenge for him. Freedom would
be enough; everything.

"Watch out for the sign," Salvatore said.

A minute later it showed in the lights as if in obedience to
his will: MONTELIANA—3 km. Then the zigzags met them,
plunging them into and raising them out of a trough, the road
finally levelling off, the drop to one side, the narrow plateau
appearing on the right.

"*Fermi, fermi.*"

Forrester pulled into the side. The road forked just ahead.

"Out, Carlo."

Carlo opened the nearside door and dropped stiffly on to the verge.

"It will be a long night," Salvatore warned him. "But don't come down into the town. Keep away. Get into the trees somewhere and wait."

Carlo's face was star-green. He hesitated. "What about Guiseppe and you?"

"We'll go on."

"But you said—"

"I've changed my mind."

Uneasily, Carlo retorted: "Don't change it over the pick-up in the morning."

"That stands. Everything else stands. I'll have joined you by then myself."

Carlo nodded. "*Ciao*, then. Good luck."

Margherita pulled the door to. Forrester headed past the fork and along the road that curved down to where Monteliana lay on the hill-shelf at the base of the cliff. Halfway down four men walked towards them in file, wheeling bicycles, and their stares seemed to imply knowledge.

"Slowly into the town," Salvatore said. The decisions were his, the plan was his; he gave the orders.

"How far are you going?"

"I'll show you."

The lights of the place came at them as if a curtain were being drawn aside; a sprinkling first, and then the main concentration, topped by the illuminated dome of the church.

Guiseppe was becoming restless. "This will do, surely?"

They were into the fringes, waste land scattered with single-storey buildings and clumps of prickly pear, hoardings and rubble. Salvatore delayed, exercising his authority, before saying: "Here."

Forrester braked. Guiseppe was out in a flash; Salvatore had

165

difficulty finding the door-handle: he wasn't accustomed to cars. Forrester leaned across and lifted the catch for him.

"Do what you have to do," Salvatore said as a parting shot, "and you will have no regrets. If it should enter your head to abandon us and drive to the hut alone I warn you it will do you and the woman no good. Luigi has been told. Either we return there together or you carry a written message from me. Which will happen I shall decide tomorrow."

Forrester glared at him, but didn't answer. Salvatore seemed to have shrunk, somehow. Standing on the edge of the road with Guiseppe beside him in his cloth cap they both seemed the very worst kind of allies, small-time bandits who had gambled and bungled once before. Only in their hold on him had they shown any skill.

"Until morning, Margherita."

A wave and they loped away, making for cover.

Music blared from a bar in the main street. A Franciscan friar flapped in sandals along the pavement. Forrester nosed the Fiat carefully through the evening strollers who spilled on to the carriageway. In the small square a crowd watched a puppet show and lovers sat in pairs on the public benches. Sunday night: normality was everywhere. He drove on through and out of the centre of things, on the alert for uniforms, dreading some fluke of chance that could, even now, bring disaster landsliding down. He made the two remembered turns, right and left, and the town began to break up again as the road to the lock-up ran parallel to the rising cliff face. The street lights ended abruptly as the untenanted stretch of scrub began and he cut his own. Peering, he could just about see his way. A scored track branched off, used by refuse carts he guessed, and he took it, bumping over the rough ground until he was close in beside the rubbish tip. With difficulty he swung the car round and reversed as far as he could go, and every loose can, every scrap of overspilled junk that crunched under the wheels, seemed to signal their arrival.

He was hard under the cliff, perhaps fifty yards from the strip of road, when he braked and switched off; the tip was between them and the lock-up. As the engine died the silence came flooding in, unnerving, more intense than he could remember, no waterfall, nothing except the stillness and the continuing sensation of movement after the drive.

In a low voice he asked Margherita: "Give me a cigarette, will you?" He'd confirmed that she had them before they'd set out. Then he remembered the explosives and said: "Forget it." Fool.

The stench of the tip seeped into the car, but he didn't stir. He felt he never wanted to move again. Suddenly a cat squealed, quite near, and his scalp seemed to contract. Still he delayed, sitting there, at war within himself.

"What's the matter?"

"Nothing," he said sharply. "*Niente*," and started to get out.

31

H E lifted the box of explosives after him and put them on the ground; pocketed the car keys. Action eased the grip on his nerves. As quietly as he could he pushed the door to. Then he went to the boot, pulled the blankets away and removed the fuse assembly and the tyre-lever. The dirt-streaked white Fiat looked dreadfully conspicuous, the windscreen's pale reflection a giveaway, and he made an effort to camouflage it. He scavenged round the base of the tip with Margherita until they found a couple of sheets of rusted corrugated iron, and these they propped across the front of the bonnet and partially along one side; the coarse blankets, spread out and weighted down, covered most of the glass.

"You take the box and the tyre-lever," he said.

They kept close to the cliff and staggered over the tip, feet sinking into God knows what. There were rats here. Forrester led. As they reached the crest the lock-up became visible, its great sandstone walls greyish under the stars. Two hundred yards. The cat squealed again, a spitting, hair-bristling sound, then bounded across them and vanished. Beyond the tip was more waste ground, dotted with scrub and bordered with rock fragments fallen from the cliff face. They must have taken five minutes to reach halfway. Every few paces Forrester paused, searching for a sign of the guard; but in vain. Once, Margherita kicked against a stone, and it dislodged others, freezing them between strides until the rattling ended.

"*Madonna!*" he heard, under her breath, and it was a comfort to him: alone, this would have been so much worse.

They covered perhaps thirty yards more. They were slightly less exposed than if they'd been out in the open, yet they were casting pale shadows; the stars were strong and there wasn't a sign of a cloud. Obliquely, the main gates were edging into view now. Just ahead there was a very slight concave depression in the base of the cliff and when they reached it Forrester indicated to Margherita to go to ground.

"Why?" she whispered.

"Several reasons."

He laid the weighty fuse assembly flat, then sat down, back to the rock.

"Why?" she repeated, settling beside him.

"First, I have to check and arm the fuses. And, second, I

168

want to time that guard." Her look disturbed him. "Hell, we've all night, haven't we?"

Something throbbed in the distance, faint to begin with, growing louder. A plane? . . . Yes. Presently Forrester saw it, not too high, a fixed pattern of lights ploughing through the quivering sky, slow-wheeling towards Palermo, he reckoned. And he thought with an immense envy of the people up there, imagining them with their final duty-free drinks, their travellers cheques and *lire*, their cameras and baggage. Whoever they were, they were his kind, Inger's kind, and nothing as nightmarish as this would happen to them.

Six minutes past eight. He could feel his heart beating against his drawn-up knees.

A dry cough was the first indication of the guard's arrival. Margherita nudged Forrester and pointed to the far corner of the lock-up wall, near the observation point. Forrester soon picked him out; he patrolled clockwise, then.

The guard ambled along the length of the wall and each gritty step on the gravel travelled as if amplified by the silence. He took his time, certainly. As he neared the gates he coughed again, then cursed quietly. At that range—sixty, seventy yards, say—he seemed to lack menace. But when he reached the gates he stopped and pulled a chair from an angle in the wall, grunted and sat down. And, as he did so, Forrester saw to his alarm that he unslung a rifle from his shoulder.

"He will stay ten minutes, then go."

Margherita continued to be adamant about this. Yet there had never been mention that the guard would be armed. Perhaps she hadn't known it—in which case she could be wrong in other directions. Anyway, Forrester was taking nothing on trust; he was going to check and check again. There was time enough.

Eight twelve. The guard lit a cigarette. They sat watching,

not moving, and they could see the red glow fade and brighten and the smoke swirl in the still air. Every minute seemed to stretch elastically into distortions of time. Now and again the guard muttered to himself. At eight-twenty he flipped the cigarette-end towards the culvert. At eight twenty-three he got up, pushed the chair into the angle of wall. Then he opened a slot in the wicket-door in the right-hand gate, poked his head inside and called in a bored voice that suggested he'd done it a million times before: "Leaving now." Was he speaking to the other guard—or to someone on duty in the reception block?

"You see?" Margherita breathed. She was talking about an enemy.

Eight twenty-five. The guard slung his rifle and proceeded on his round. He'd turned into view at nine minutes past, and now he reached the near corner at exactly eight twenty-seven: they would therefore be exposed to him for anything up to twenty minutes at a stretch, twenty minutes in every hour.

"Is he relieved?"

"At midnight."

She seemed to expect Forrester to make a move there and then; indeed she rose herself and picked up the box. But he shook his head.

"Not yet."

"We can get closer."

"This is fine where we are. I've got plenty to do first. Besides, I'm timing him again. And another thing—the later we finish the better it will be."

He uncoiled the fuse assembly and spread it out; from end to end it stretched all of fifty feet. The detonators were in his shirt pockets, wrapped in handkerchiefs, and he put these on the ground also, together with the binding tape. Then he opened the box and removed the first of the twelve made-up charges. Margherita watched him intently. With expert care he began arming the fuse-ends—a detonator first, crimping it with his teeth until the open end bit into the fuse, then inserting the detonator into the explosive, sandwiching it between the double slabs, finally taping it firmly into position. The starlight was wonderfully strong; too strong.

"The charge has to lie flush against the metal," he reminded Margherita, demonstrating with the palm of his hand as if it were a hinge. "Remember that."

She nodded, continuing to watch him. "How long will you be?"

"A goodish while."

"What can I do?" Already she was impatient.

"Nothing."

"There must be something. I could go over to the culvert."

"Not yet."

"I could leave the bar there." She meant the tyre-lever.

"No."

"The culvert may be blocked. It could need clearing."

"Let the guard come round again. Wait, for God's sake."

Somewhere in the distance a dog was yapping. Forrester armed three more of the fuse-ends. He could feel Margherita's hostility. Was caution so stupid? There would be risks enough before the night was out. From the moment they left the background of the cliff they would be living with danger. He paused before crimping another detonator and gazed across the short expanse of scrubland, picturing the two of them at work right under the gates, entrenching the fuses, running them up to the hinges on either side and taping them on, Margherita balanced on his shoulders for the uppermost pair . . . Only now was he aware how demanding these risks would be. They had scarcely begun to sap him.

32

THE guard re-appeared at precisely five past nine. So his tour took less than an hour; he wasn't as like clockwork as Margherita had made out. But his ritual was much the same—the leisurely approach, the break to rest his feet, the cigarette. He was younger than Forrester had supposed; he sang quietly to himself as he lolled on the chair and it wasn't an old voice. This time, instead of opening the slot in the wicket-door he twice rapped the rifle-butt against the gate and called: "Going round." All in all he remained in view for twenty-one minutes.

Reluctantly Forrester got to his feet. He couldn't reasonably delay any more. The fuse assembly was completely armed, ready, but he wouldn't move it until later. One thing at a time. Margherita was right about the culvert; it had to be inspected first, and it was up to him to do it.

"You stay here," he said. "There's no sense in both of us going."

He took the tyre-lever from her. Instinctively he crouched as he went forward. The stunted bushes dotting the hard, stony soil were no more than knee-high. He covered the first twenty yards at a walk, stepping into the dwarfed ghost of his shadow, eyes darting left and right. Nothing moved except him, there were no sounds except his own. Then a small bird got up from almost under his feet and flipped away in terror. Every muscle in Forrester's body seemed to seize. He was approaching the culvert diagonally, more than halfway there, another twenty-five yards to go, when without warning the wicket-door suddenly opened. Forrester went down as though he'd been tripped, jarring against the ground. A man came out, shut the door behind him, crossed the culvert and turned along the strip of road towards the town. A glance in Forrester's direction and he must have seen him, but he raised his jacket collar as he passed and went on his way, whistling. Civilian clothes; someone coming off duty? Forrester peered at his watch; just after the half-hour. God, he hadn't reckoned on interruption except from the guard; and it could happen again—at any moment.

Shaken, he watched the man dwindle; little by little the starlight dissolved him. It wasn't easy to get up again. Bent low, as if under cross-fire, he hurried through the last of the scrub. Grit crackled underfoot as he crossed the road and the sense of exposure was overpowering. The ditch was deceptively deep and he staggered down its bank to the open end of the culvert, the gates hardly more than twenty feet away, the walls towering. It was a brick culvert, square shaped, wide enough to take them both but silted, partially blocked with dead thorn wood and heaps of detritus, a faint glimmer showing through from the other end.

He squirmed in, and the tyre-lever struck against the brick-work with a hard, ringing sound. It was pitch black inside: something springy brushed his face and he clawed it away. He could just about crouch on hands and knees under the low roof. Moss-covered sides, dried slush and muck beneath him. As a refuge it would serve, but the air was foul and for a few claustrophobic seconds he struggled for breath. With difficulty he managed to turn himself round so that he faced outwards; the small noises as he did so seemed to megaphone past him into the open.

Looking back under his right armpit he could see a bush partly screening the other end. All to the good. He groped about, fingers like antennae, trying to establish shape and substance, clearing the culvert of everything loose that might rattle and betray them; it was going to be a tight fit with

173

Margherita in there as well. What next? He paused, hesitating. Either he went out and examined the gates and the ground where the fuses had to be buried, or he returned to the cliff-face for the assembly. Both had to be done, but time was a factor. He made it almost quarter to ten, which meant the guard had completed almost half his circuit. Going back would be wiser—and easier. He couldn't steel himself for the other thing yet.

He laid the tyre-lever close in to the side and wriggled clear. If the wicket-door opened now he was finished. A diffused glow showed above the town, but the road was deserted. He scrambled out of the ditch, tip-toed across the road and headed through the scrub, and with every step his nerves were braced for a shout from behind, a challenge.

"Here," Margherita whispered, rising from the ground. "Over here."

He had gone off line. He came along the base of the cliff to where she was and squatted beside her, breathing hard, his face glistening.

"How is it?"

"Not bad. Could be worse."

"What now?"

"We get this over there."

Forrester began looping the assembly into manageable size, careful not to disturb the junctions or tangle the leads. The dark of the culvert was no place for repairs or involved unravelling. With the charges taped on it was considerably heavier and more unwieldy than before.

"You'll have to help me carry this."

Once again he looked at his watch; they had just about long enough before the guard's return. He lifted the end where the charges were bundled and Margherita took the other.

"For God's sake watch out for someone else coming through the gate . . . Ready?"

174

She nodded. They went side by side, cradling the assembly between them, moving slower than when Forrester had been alone. A tiny part of his mind registered the fact that a flock of small clouds had gathered low in the south-west, but this was only a fleeting, almost unconscious distraction. He was back in a no-man's-land where stealth and tension were the measure. They reached the road without incident. He thought they were going to be all right then, but as they made for the ditch they heard the guard's dry cough and for one awful moment Forrester almost panicked.

"Quick!"

They all-but lost their balance in the frantic stumble down the slope to the culvert. Anyone on the alert inside the gates could hardly have missed the disturbance. Whether the guard had turned the corner Forrester didn't know, and he wasn't waiting to check. Crouching he hissed: "Get in! Get in!"

Margherita didn't need telling; she disappeared head first, dragging the assembly after her. As soon as her legs vanished Forrester followed, sculling on his elbows, the two of them creating an almost continuous resonance. Her feet struck him in the face and he bit his lip to seal the grunt of pain. But he was in, desperately sliding the last of the fuse alongside—or trying to. Suddenly it went taut in his hands and wouldn't move.

Stuck, the charges caught on something.

He started to swivel round, contorting himself in the narrow tunnel, hoping to release them, but the guard coughed again, from along the wall now, and Forrester knew it could be fatal to move another inch. And he dare not tug the fuse any more in case he damaged the connections. Peering through the blood-beat in his eyes he could just discern the darkish bundle of charges protruding into the starlit ditch.

The guard's footstep crunched on the path below the wall. "Where is he?" he wanted to ask; Margherita could probably

175

see him. Then, as if she read his mind, he felt the pressure of a shoe against his neck. Close, very close, a stone's-throw. In despair he made one more furtive attempt to free the charges, twisting until he thought the muscles in his back would snap, reaching as far as he possibly could, but in vain.

"Ayee," they heard the guard sigh, and the sound funnelled in to them. Footsteps, the scrape of the chair being shifted, an unintelligible mutter, another cough, then the strike of a match.

They lay absolutely still, and already Forrester knew the next few minutes would seem to last for ever. The guard hummed quietly to himself, occasionally tapping his feet. Once he exclaimed "*Madre!*" as if he were sick with boredom and the endless routine. Inside the culvert they could only guess— guess at that, and guess at the meaning of the silences. Drawing on his cigarette? Staring at the stars? Suspicious, suddenly— some instinct alerted? . . . The silences were the worst to bear, prodding the imagination. How many times would they have to endure this before dawn? Eight? Nine? . . . Forrester's mouth began to twitch. There was so little air.

At last the guard moved again. Yawning, he stood up. And all at once a shower of sparks cascaded over Forrester's end of the culvert, dying as they drifted down to the explosives. The guard swore quietly and walked forward, his footsteps vibrating through the brickwork. Immediately above them he stopped, heeling out the lighted cigarette-stub and it was beyond Forrester's understanding how it was that he didn't notice the dull glint of the aluminium detonators jutting from the charges, or the charges themselves.

A rough, grating sound, and the stub was swept over into the ditch. Then, after an age, the footsteps retreated. Thump, thump on the gate. "On my way."

And relief broke through Forrester like a dam bursting, dribbles of sweat salting his lips.

33

H E watched the guard saunter to the corner of the lock-up that was visible from his side; he could see nothing of the man below the waist, only the shoulders and capped head and the barrel of the slung rifle, a soft silhouette against the wall.

"Has he gone?"

"Not yet."

His mouth was so dry he could hardly form the words. He waited, and even when the guard had turned out of sight he went on waiting, nausea fluttering in his stomach as the tension throbbed slowly out of him.

"Gone now?"

"Yes."

Margherita shifted round to face him; small, compact, it was easier for her.

Forrester whispered: "We nearly had it then." He edged to the culvert's entrance and released the charges: they were caught behind tufts of weed, but the junctions were intact as far as he could tell.

"What next?"

Her eagerness appalled him. She seemed to be quite without nerves, indifferent to a skin-of-the-teeth reprieve. His hands were shaking as he lifted the charges inside, paying the fuses back as he did so.

With a kind of rebellion he answered: "We sort this lot out, that's what."

His eyes had adjusted to the darkness; no longer was he groping. He brought the thick central stem of the assembly to the centre of the culvert and began fanning the leads left and right, six to one side, six to the other, moving them with great care. It was enormously difficult, the space too cramped, the leads too long. They still had to be doubled back and forth, yet at all costs they mustn't be crossed or twisted; when the time came to run them out they would have to flow cleanly, without a hitch.

Eventually, Forrester was satisfied. But again there was that awful disinclination to leave cover and proceed to the next stage. Yet he had no choice, and something Salvatore had said returned to goad him—"What a man does when it matters is the important thing."

"This way," he breathed to Margherita. "Don't ever use that side—the bush there's good camouflage."

She followed him, bringing the tyre-lever, crossing herself as she emerged. They crouched in the ditch, the massive iron-studded gates seeming to rise sheer above them, the wicket-door like a trap that could spring them to disaster. To test the ground he took the lever and began to score a shallow trench up the side of the ditch—half an inch or so deep, half an inch wide. Here, at least, the surface was yielding enough, dry and flakey, and the metal cut easily. Back at the hut he had demonstrated what was required, and now, returning the lever to Margherita, he mimed instructions. No farther than the top of the bank. Keep the channel straight . . . Yes? Head tilted. Yes? . . . Then the same at the other end of the culvert . . . *D'accordo?*

He left her and crept out of the ditch. Twelve to fourteen feet separated him from the gates, four to five strides, yet it must have taken him all of a minute to reach them. He kept to the rough verge beside the tarmac strip, transferring his weight from leg to leg with the caution of someone moving on thin ice.

The gates were set slightly back from the end pillars of the wall, and the chair the guard used stood in the recess on the right. Forrester slid into the one on the left and began to examine the heavy strap hinges; with relief he saw that they presented no unexpected difficulties. Through the narrow gap between wall and gate he could just make out the squat shape of the reception block: it was about ten yards away. A light glowed in the end window, but there was no sign of occupation; nor could Forrester see or hear anything of the guard who was said to patrol the lock-up grounds. Inside, everything was deathly quiet, but twice behind him Margherita struck stone and to him the tiny sound seemed enormous, making him wince with alarm.

He studied the hinges once more, professionally satisfied that he hadn't under-estimated the weight of explosive; they were old and rusted and would sheer through without trouble. This was a gamble which could be—and had been—calculated. But the long-drawn business of placing the charges and burying the fuses could not, and then in the last resort the success of the demolition was going to hang on whether the guard was observant enough to notice either what was taped to the hinges or the fuses branching up the recessed sections of the wall.

Forrester sidled clear and stepped back, searching the sky beyond the sandstone arch for the clouds he had seen an hour ago, willing them to thicken, drift, kill the tell-tale brightness. There was time yet, though not too much; he couldn't delay beyond one o'clock, and already it was nearing eleven.

He felt the corner of his mouth twitch again. For a few seconds he seemed unable to move; without cause, a kind of paralysis. Just the starlight and the silence and the reason for being there, all at work on his imagination—like the night he and Corporal Dunbar patrolled and lost one another and he was isolated for an hour, watching by the stream and believing himself watched, closed in upon. But the past didn't help or belong here.

He shivered and turned, the grip on him broken. Someone was talking inside the lock-up; someone walking. He went on his toes to the ditch and hurried down. Margherita was bent like a reaper at the other end of the culvert and he signalled to her urgently. She came at once, darting across the tarmac, and dropped beside him.

In, he motioned. *In* . . .

"The guard?"

"Over the gate. Two of them."

They waited, crouching in the dark space, hearing the sound of their own breath but nothing more. False alarm.

"Did you finish?" Forrester asked.

"Nearly."

Gingerly he shoved his head outside. Camouflaged by tufts of weeds the shallow channel Margherita had made was hardly noticeable; it might have been an ant-trail.

"Listen," he whispered. "The guard's due back in a matter of minutes. According to you he's relieved at midnight."

"Yes."

"We won't move again until the change is made and the new man has completed his first circuit."

"But—"

"To be on the safe side. If this one goes off duty at twelve you can bet he will vary his routine. And his relief may not keep to the same schedule."

"He does. Until eight in the morning."

She wouldn't have been able to see his shrug. "Even so we're going to wait."

"For two hours?"

"If need be. There may be some clouds by then to—"

"But that is madness." Her tone was aggressive; scornful.

"The whole thing is madness. What I'm trying to do is inject a bit of sane common sense—"

"Is it that?" she snapped, the whisper echoing about the culvert.

"Your trouble is that you don't know what patience is. None

of you do. D'you want Angelo out of there or don't you? All right. You're doing this because of him and I'm doing it for someone else. So it's got to work. It's going to work. But *my* way, minimising the risks."

He twisted away from her. Needlessly, his fingers ran about the fuse assembly as if it were the one thing he could trust. "Is it that?"—what did she mean? That patience could be used as an excuse? He did not like to be analysed, probed, his reasons doubted. He knew his weaknesses, and they were natural enough; but he had never failed to master them—and would again. A matter of hours from now and this girl would have left his life for ever. Until then he needed her, but why should he care what she thought or how she judged him? Inger, yes— that was something different.

34

THE guard reached the gate soon after eleven; Forrester didn't check the exact time. They lay doubled up in the culvert listening to every move he made, every sound he uttered. The air seemed more stifling, more dust-laden, as the minutes crawled by, and Forrester dreaded that he would sneeze or reflexively clear his throat. He tried to calm himself by letting his thoughts go free, away from here and the pulsing beat of his heart's measurement of time.

Had Carlo had them under observation from the cliff-top? What were the others doing? . . . And Inger? Most of all Inger.

A faint swishing suddenly reached his ears. Mystified, he looked down the ditch and to his horror he saw a dog loping along its bank. He caught Margherita by the arm and drew her close, lips pressed into her hair, mouthing the warning. He was blocking her view.

"*Cane.*"

A bitch, skin and bone, like a greyhound, teats swinging. Jesus, if it came to the culvert . . . As if mesmerised Forrester watched it sniff hungrily about among the weeds, pause, urinate and move nearer. Then the guard saved them.

"Go away ! . . . Hey ! Hey ! . . . Off with you !"

The bitch halted, ears flattened. There was a scraping noise by the gates as if the guard had jumped to his feet.

"Good-for-nothing."

A stone clipped into the ground. The bitch spun round and scurried away, bounded over the ditch and vanished.

"Yaaah," the guard growled, settling back on to his chair. "Filth, you."

Relief see-sawed down through Forrester again; under the skin his flesh tingled. Their luck was holding. He touched Margherita, conveying that the danger had passed. Long, spun-out minutes elapsed. When he shifted his weight from one bent arm to another the elbow seemed to crack like a pistol-shot.

The guard was in no hurry to get going. And when at last he chose to dispense with the chair he didn't stray far from the gates. He patrolled the front wall only, back and forth a couple of times, cap askew, yawning frequently, covered all the way by either Forrester or Margherita according to which side of the gates he was. Towards twelve Forrester saw the leading edge of packed cloud beginning imperceptibly to push northwards above the lock-up wall and he stared up at it in thankfulness. It was coming at the right time, but when it had spread over and the worst of the light had gone the worry would be that the cloud wouldn't last. The starshine had reached a peak now; he could make out details of the guard's shabby uniform and the narrow, lop-sided features.

At midnight sharp the wicket-door opened. They heard the bolt pulled, the door creak and someone step through.

"*Ciao, Silvio,*" the newcomer said without enthusiasm. "How's it gone?" Older this one; gruff.

"As usual."

"Nothing?"

"One of these nights I'll surprise you and say there was." The first guard chuckled. "Smoke?"

Sometimes their words carried into the culvert, sometimes not. They remained together for a while, a habit obviously, until the first one decided there was a better place to be.

" 'Night, then."

"*Ciao.*"

"Cheer up. It's a living."

The new man made a coarse noise: you could joke when your stint was done. The door creaked to and the bolt was rammed home. Without waiting the guard set off on patrol, clock-wise again, his pace a shade quicker than the other's. Forrester followed him with his eyes—short, fat, with a sailor's roll. And at last he and Margherita could relax, stretch their numbed limbs, speak.

"Surely I could finish the bank on my side?"

"Is there much to do?"

"I told you, no."

"I'll see to it." A few minutes only; he could chance that.

"And then?"

"In an hour, or as soon after as possible, we tackle the right hand set of hinges. You can complete the channel all the way to the recess in the wall, lay the leads in and bury them. By the time you've done that I'll be ready for your help on the top hinge. We'll need to work fast. There ought to be some cloud

183

cover, which will help, but twenty to twenty-five minutes should be about long enough."

He crawled into the ditch with the tyre-lever. The pinkish sky-glow over the town had dimmed a little, but the mottled clouds hardly seemed to have shifted. For a second or two before clambering out of the ditch Forrester looked over towards the refuse-tip, tempted again by the comparative nearness of the car, the keys in his pocket. Margherita was powerless; she wasn't armed. But Luigi was, and whether he could cope with him, surprise him at the hut, was really all that stood between his breaking away—and had done from the start. Salvatore had foreseen this gap in his hold on him and warned Luigi, purposely left him the shot-gun. And if there was no certainty of surprise, no trick by which Luigi could be taken unawares, he would demand Salvatore's written proof that all was well. "D'you take us for fools, friend? . . ."

For a long moment the choice swung like a pendulum before Forrester turned and made his way cautiously across the tarmac strip to the ditch at the culvert's other end. Better the risks you knew; at least they carried what passed for a guarantee.

Margherita had left only a few feet of trench to be scratched out. He set to work, facing the gates, urban senses strained to the limit. He wasn't long in finishing, but danger was never more than a blink away and gnawed at his nerves. There had been other times like this—with Dunbar, with Singer; the past refused to lie down.

When he had cut to the top of bank where the weeds ended he came straight back to the culvert and wriggled in.

"What time is it?"

"About twenty to."

Not much more than another half hour to wait before the gamble began in earnest. Sweating, Forrester lay curled in the tight space. His stomach grumbled with hunger he didn't feel.

184

He screwed his head to one side and stared out and up, praying for the clouds.

The light began to thicken not long before the new guard completed his first tour. They heard his gritty approach from the far corner of the wall at three minutes after the hour; he was more of a time-keeper. When he reached the gates he made use of the chair, but only briefly: he was soon on his feet again, circling aimlessly, idly kicking at stones, as if he found moving about lessened the inevitable tedium.

Inside the culvert they dared not move. The night seemed to be shrinking and Forrester knew that the clouds were hazing over at last. Not before time, but the luck was lasting like a dream. So far . . . All the way, for Christ's sake, *all* the way.

The chair was pushed aside. One fifteen . . . Now the worst was coming. The guard shuffled off, head and shoulders rolling as he passed along the wall. Forrester waited until he had turned the corner.

"Yes?" Margherita breathed, moving already. She wouldn't spare herself.

He held up a hand, part warning, part signal, forgetting she wouldn't see it. Ten or fifteen seconds more, the night's silence flowing back, one risk receding.

"Yes?"—almost inaudibly.

"Yes," he answered thickly. "Come on."

35

H E crept immediately to the far side of the culvert where the bush was and pulled the right-hand leads of the fuse-assembly out. They came freely, like well-coiled cord, the main lead a single stem of fuse that only branched into six over the last quarter of its length. He backed up the bank and then went sideways towards the gates, stepping as if his feet pained him. It was decidedly darker, the clouds like ice-floes. He moved the guard's chair, eased into the wall recess and squinted through the gap, getting a direct view of the lighted window in the reception block; it framed a shirt-sleeved man reading a newspaper. Roughly, Forrester measured the fuse branches against the distance between hinges and found he'd estimated well; not too little, only a shade too much. Glancing round he then saw that Margherita was first scraping a guide-line across the level ground and the path the guard used. He withdrew until he was beside her and with his mouth to the shell of her ear told her to pull back what slack there was on the main stem. This she did, tugging gently from the mouth of the culvert until the fuse lay straight across the ground.

For hours the binding-tape had pressed against Forrester's left thigh. Now he crouched in the recess and started taping the two lowest charges. The straps of the hinges joined as they left the wood, angling sharply from back and front of the gate, narrowing down, metal to metal. The light seemed to be going all the time, but he could just about see, and in any case he was skilled enough to have done this blindfold. The charges fitted snugly against the hinge and there was an adequate gap to put his hands through when stringing the tape round. Again and again he lifted his eyes nervously to the lighted window; it was half open, and when the man turned the newspaper the rustle sounded crisp and clear. In places Margherita was having to chip gently at the ground and the noise, small though it was, undermined Forrester's hard-held control. Was the man deaf in there?

He straightened: the middle hinge he could manage standing, reaching up. He guided the second pair of fuse branches up the wall by way of fissures between the worn sandstone blocks, doing his best to hide their presence. The black tape and the chocolate-brown slabs merged well with the rusted metal— at least while the clouds dulled everything down—but the fuses would be there for anyone with eyes to see. At dawn, too.

The first of the second two charges was in position when the man on duty tossed the paper aside, stood up and came to the window. For an appalled moment Forrester believed he had heard something; lips parted, stock still, he squinted through the gap. But the man pulled the window to and shut it, as if the night air was now too sharp for him. For Forrester there was no such chill; a sweaty fever seemed to be on him. He sucked in breath and taped the other charge into position on the reverse side of the hinge, separating them by about half an inch to produce a shearing effect, fingers shaking as he ran the tape over.

Margherita had worked to within a yard or so of him. One thirty-five . . . He left the last two charges dangling and edged out of the recess to give her room, everything in him urging her to hurry, and every strike on stone, every granular crunch as she moved, made him want to tear the lever from her and complete the job himself.

At last she finished. In dumb-show he instructed her to prop the lever against the wall and climb on to his shoulders. The chair wouldn't give him the necessary height. He stooped to receive her, hauling her up until her feet straddled his neck.

Awkwardly, using the wall to keep balanced, he sidled into the recess and passed up the tape, then the first of the remaining leads, relying on her now, wishing he could repeat his instructions yet not daring to, eyeing the man in the window ten bare yards away, Margherita's legs against his ears, partially blocking his hearing.

He seemed to bear her weight for an impossibly long time before she kicked him gently on the shoulder to indicate that she needed the second charge. He passed it up and waited, fretting the minutes through. Quarter to? . . . Ten to? . . . Come on, his mind said. Come *on* . . . Then she kicked him again and, bending, reached down with the tape. He backed out of the recess and leaned so that she could scramble off his back. No sooner had she separated from him than he was miming at her again to start entrenching the main fuse. She nodded and began at once, crouching, slotting it into the scratched-out channel and covering it over.

Forrester gazed up at the charges she had placed; they looked all right. Here and there he was again able to bend a fuse-lead into a wall crevice, but some were at impossible angles, so he licked his fingers, ran the wet along the leads and showered them with dust scooped from the recess, doing this repeatedly, masticating spittle on to his tongue, transferring the taste of the explosive to his mouth until he could bear it no more.

Gently he lifted the chair back into the recess. For the last time he tip-toed away from the right-hand gate. The man in the window was drinking from an enamel mug. Margherita had worked two-thirds of the way to the ditch. Forrester picked up the tyre-lever and moved behind her, treading the re-packed earth a shade firmer. When she reached the ditch he went past her and roughly buried the fuse into the shallow cut, not so carefully here where weeds and an uneven surface made natural camouflage.

188

"Ready?" he whispered presently, risking his voice, and she nodded. Calmly she crossed the tarmac strip and he followed her down the other side and back into the culvert where his heart hammered as if it were in an echo-chamber and the bitter-sweet stench from his hands made him want to retch.

Seven minutes to two. They'd taken longer than he had bargained for, but now it was done it seemed like a miracle that they should have got away with it without a hitch.

"That was good, eh?" There was something like elation in Margherita's voice. "All right?"

"All right, yes." Forrester swallowed, mouth dry, sweat pumping in greasy streams. "Now there's just one more time."

36

AGAIN they waited for the guard. There had been so much waiting, and there was plenty still to come, but from now on there was a difference. From now on, with hourly regularity, they had to trust in the guard's blindness, instinctive and otherwise, to the fact that something might be wrong.

He was round at five minutes after two. There must be other stopping-points, Forrester decided; if this one kept to his rolling pace for three-quarters of an hour he would circle the lock-up at least twice. Perhaps he delayed at the service and chapel gates on his way. Not that it mattered what he did, where he went. Nothing mattered except the regularity of his

189

absence from the north wall and the blunting effect of boredom whenever he was here.

They heard him drag the chair forward and subside, the thump of his rifle-butt. Five times now they had strained and listened, deciphering the meaning of sounds, but as always the silences prickled the nerves. Was he sniffing, having caught the very slightest whiff of the explosive? Hardly—and yet . . . Staring at the ground between his feet, curious about some loose soil? God alone knew. They could only wait and hope, afraid to stir, willing him to get up and mooch away again. Had Margherita known what it would be like? Not once had she faltered.

At two-fifteen the guard sighed and lifted his rifle—they heard the slap of the sling. Then he rose and shoved the chair back in the recess. If he were going to notice anything it could be then, but no. Unlike his colleague he didn't signal his departure by banging the gates. Watching, Forrester dimly saw him move along the top of the bank: thank God for the clouds, the night was all shadow now.

One more time . . .

He gave the guard a minute, then wriggled into the open and dragged the other half of the assembly after him, paying it out as he climbed the bank. They had a pattern to follow, a successful drill, but this time he found it harder, harder because he was clumsy, harder because he seemed to have depleted himself already, harder because he couldn't observe the man in the window and use him as a partial safety-gauge. In every way more jittery, less efficient, more prey to speculation. And slower, every error time-consuming.

Twice he botched taping the bottom charges. Once the tape dropped from his fingers and only by reaching through at arm's-length did he retrieve it from the other side of the gate. And at one point Margherita jarred the tyre-lever so heavily against rock that fear clutched at his throat. He managed the

190

middle hinge better, though still like a novice, vital minutes slipping away. A crossed lead, an insecure detonator . . . They were cutting it desperately fine. Margherita had finished gouging the channel well before he was ready for her and so she started burying the fuse, covering it loosely with her hands, then treading it down. She was into the ditch when he signalled her.

Almost three . . . Frantically he hauled her on to his shoulders and edged into the recess. They could still make it. A few minutes more. The tape and one of the charges handed up. Hurry, hurry, for Christ's sake . . .

And then with a stab of terror that seemed to disintegrate his mind Forrester heard the guard on the path only yards away.

All control went in the first elemental rush of panic. He started to twist clear, about to run, meaning to run, but Margherita prevented him—not only her weight on his shoulders but the hissed command.

"Don't move!"

Suddenly, in contrast, he was petrified, his brain numb. Crunch, crunch, on the stony path. There had been no warning. Forrester's insides seemed to be dribbling away, his legs trembling, Margherita motionless above him. Together they leaned into the dark within the dark, faces to the corner. The guard sauntered to a standstill when he was level with the gates, broke wind, then dragged the chair from the other recess. It was beyond belief that he hadn't seen them. He was terribly close; they could hear his rasped breathing, the dry sound of his hands being rubbed together, the small pressure-creaks of the chair as his weight was shifted.

Time seemed to have run to a stop for Forrester. As if in a coma he remained motionless, muscles quivering in legs and arms but the rest of him still frozen, scarcely conscious of

191

Margherita's weight and the bite of her heels into his shoulders. Eyes shut, taking air through the mouth, pulse like a pile-driver.

"A lot of fools," the guard complained, abruptly giving vent to some private grievance. "They should have known."

The suddenness of his voice raised the hairs on Forrester's neck. Sweat stung his eyes when he opened them. Dimly, the remaining charge dangled in front of him on its length of fuse. Simultaneously time started to pick up again, his mind beginning to clear. Margherita's legs had his head in a vice and he couldn't shift it, couldn't risk a slight turning motion to look round. With heightened awareness he heard a blob of sweat plop on to his shoe, then another. He tensed from some reaction from the guard, but nothing happened—no scuffling of feet that could follow a searching sidelong glance, no alarmed snatching for the rifle.

"Camillo," the man muttered, "you bastard, you . . . *Bastardo*," he repeated with relish.

Margherita remained like a statue. How long? Five minutes? And how much longer? It couldn't last. Forrester gritted his teeth. For a drawn-out moment the starlight seemed to swell, as if coming again, but the dark held steady. On and on, not a movement from them, wire taut, the charge close to Forrester's face bouncing in and out of focus with every beat of his heart. Far off, a dog was barking somewhere. The smell of the explosive hung in the recess. Behind him, the chair creaked and creaked again. More leaking drips of sweat. His thoughts were going frantically in all directions at once. Thank God she'd buried the fuses: it would have ended already but for that . . .

Silence, time crawling by. Dust in the mouth, nerves pricking needle-points of ice and fire. And something rising slowly within him like a bubble in oil, something unidentified, waiting to surface as soon as the tension snapped. Either way.

The guard whistled softly to himself, feet tapping a gritty rhythm. Another minute, another lifetime. Then, as suddenly as he had arrived, he decided to go. He got up and dragged the chair back to its usual place. Forrester cringed: now it would come, now. Shapes in the far recess, shadows amongst shadows —the man *must* see . . . But with disbelief he heard him sling his rifle, cross the tarmac strip and start along the path beyond the end pillar of the wall.

A shudder surged through Forrester from head to toe, but neither he nor Margherita moved. Then, furtively, as if on a signal, they both eased their positions slightly. No word was exchanged. They continued to wait for an unnecessarily long time after the guard had gone, as if they still couldn't accept their escape. Presently, though, Forrester felt Margherita reaching down for the last charge and he passed it up.

Relief was so intense that he was close to vomiting. In a daze, when Margherita had taped the charge and clambered off his back, he trained the leads into the wall crevices, wet them and powdered them with dust. By the time he turned to retreat she had already re-trodden any tell-tale blemishes where the fuses were entrenched and was waiting for him in the ditch.

"Mother of God," she said solemnly, but nothing more; not then.

He followed her into the culvert. Did she know? He would have run. When the blind panic severed his mind and body every instinct was to run, abandon her, abandon everything except himself. Run. Did she know? All along he'd known, minute by minute standing there, sweating and fearful. But only as he came to join her, only just now, did the surfacing bubble burst and the realisation hit him that he had panicked before. Twice. And neither time had there been anyone to stop him.

He curled in the culvert with his face to the air, the relief forgotten, the tension forgotten.

Twice ... Yes. *Yes.*

37

D UG in on the hill, the hill almost bare because of the shelling, what trees there were like white sticks, stripped of bark, the mud-green river below them beyond the wire, hills to both sides, not pimples like this one, and the road somewhere hidden on the right and the Australians beyond it and beyond them the Americans. Evening, and Singer, his head bandaged, the bandage black with blood, crawling in to say: "They'll probably throw a feint at us here and put their main thrust in along the valley. That's as maybe, but whichever way the cat jumps we're to hold as long as possible ... Good luck, Neal."

Night then, and the shelling and the raking tracer-guided fire from across the tight valley, smashing the wire and preventing any repairs. An early moon, soon gone. An attack before dawn as the mortars lifted, the Chinese coming in waves and beginning to get through, outnumbering them, screaming as they blundered through the litter of their own dead, the long bayonets in the grey light. And then the light becoming day, the red sun through the smoke, but the hill still theirs—all morning remaining theirs, what was left of them. Rowell dead, Corporal McCann dead, Cole and Ireland dead, Dunbar as good as—"My legs, sir! Jesus, my legs!" Eleven others wounded, no stretcher-bearers, contact lost with headquarters and the flanking platoons and only seven men still in action. More mortaring, and another attack, just held, grenade for grenade, followed by the unaccountable pause, the deafened silence with the bitter smoke clearing. And with the silence the panic, the glazed getting to his feet and walking away, realising that others followed—two, three, four: four, yes, and not caring who, not really knowing who, until late in the afternoon when he reached the reserve lines.

Lying in a culvert at Monteliana and remembering all this, seeing himself as he once was, tonight's panic bridging the years and tearing the veils aside for the very first time. LOCAL MAN WINS M.C. IN KOREA . . . Coming home to the unreality of everything, nothing the same though intrinsically unchanged, the truth of a single moment blurred by the culmination of a night and morning's pounding shock and incoherence, and never clarified, never recaptured. Coming home to that pompous champagne party and the handshakes, the congratulations, the gradual shaping of an image that Diana accepted and fostered: they had met about then.

Diana . . . Unseeing, Forrester stared along the ditch towards the sleeping town. When the shale started shifting under his feet as he reached for her there had been another self-same moment, an instant of utter terror, making him draw back. Vividly, the scene overlaid his vision. Reaching for her, their fingers separated only by inches, gasping "Hold on! Hold on!" And then the loss of a foothold, the cold gust of fear and the cowardly pulling away from inches to feet, ankle-deep in the sliding surface of the hill, the shale spilling out over the cliff and Diana's eyes never leaving his. Hopelessly trying again, outstretched, fingers almost touching only to see her swept suddenly into the ravine.

He clenched his hands, bewildered. Twice . . . And now tonight—and, because of tonight, linked to the other times;

195

shamed. His mind teemed with mocking images of himself, all bluff and bravado, ignorant of the flaw, the weakness now exposed like pus hidden from him by the scars and the healed memories.

But for Margherita he would have succumbed again; a split second and it would have been too late.

She was whispering to him about Angelo, the future all that mattered, a dream nearing fulfilment. "In a week we shall be on the mainland. And then, perhaps, America. The boys have a cousin in America . . ." Eagerness in the low-pitched voice, the past dead and gone, finished with, the memories cruel but entire, honest.

Forrester barely heard her. He shivered; the sweat which drenched his shirt was cold, but he shivered because of himself: he felt old and weary and chilled in the very centre of his heart. Was he such a sham? Could he have saved Diana?— no. Could they have held that hill?—no. Neither. Again and again and again he asked himself. No . . . But those weren't the questions. Who was he? What was he built around? They were the ones.

The guard came and went once more.

"Soon it will be the others' turn."

Forrester didn't reply. Automatically, he massaged the bruised muscles at the base of his neck. *When his company had been all but over-run and his own platoon position was no longer tenable, Lieutenant Forrester withdrew the remnants of his men* . . . But for the citation and the decoration in its silk-padded box and the proclamation of it on his business-card, he might have been like other men, long since found out, their vulnerability self-acknowledged. Or there might have been someone other than his father to whom to go, someone other than Diana, and thus to have discovered himself that

196

way, cracking the myth and the hard shell that formed protectively around it. Instead of which he had had to wait until now, here, in another country and allied to strangers whose world had forged them differently and permitted them no illusions.

"*Che ora?*"

"Ten to five."

With an effort Forrester screwed his mind to meet the coming crisis. Ten to five. "At five I deal with the priest. At five-thirty Guiseppe and I enter the lock-up by the chapel gate"—Salvatore's words had the ring of something recalled after waking. Salvatore, Guiseppe, Carlo, Luigi . . .

Inger . . .

Forrester stretched himself as best he could. An hour and a half more. Away in the town the cocks were beginning to crow in the false dawn.

38

THE first glimmer of light would test the camouflage, but chance must take its course. The guard had only one more turn to make before Forrester got the signal from the cliff. The main risks were elsewhere now. Already the raid was under way—five forty; Salvatore and Guiseppe would be inside. They must have got to the chapel gate round by the south wall; there had been no sign of anyone along this side, no sound except the guard's, only the night and the dawn slowly forming as the clouds thinned.

197

"Listen," Forrester told Margherita. "The instantaneous fuse could burst our eardrums in a confined space like this. We'll have a ten-second delay after ignition, exactly ten. The guard will have moved away by six-thirty but we'll still have to keep under cover until the very last. So be ready to run for it the moment I ignite—up the bank and towards the cliff."

In the dimness of the culvert he saw her nod.

"You'd better let me have the cigarettes and matches."

He took them from her, then began checking over the thick multi-fuse stem from which the long leads led out both ends of the culvert and into which the safety-fuse and initiating detonators were set. He must have done this a dozen times already during the night.

"Is it six yet?"

"Quarter to."

Angelo ostensibly confessing; Salvatore at the cell door acting out his sin. No noise within the walls, no commotion: the house of cards hadn't collapsed yet . . . Quietly, Forrester shifted position, easing his cramped limbs, following the plan through in his mind: now and then gabbled snatches of prayer left Margherita's lips. Something was about to begin for her, nearing its end for him. "The priest comes and goes without restraint, and so shall I . . ." In Monteliana a bell began to clang.

Every time Forrester peered at his watch it hardly seemed to have moved on. An age passed before they heard the guard traipse round the far corner. Three minutes after six . . . The darkness was draining rapidly, colours seeping back. They heard the guard yawn as he sat down; idly he began pitching pebbles at a rusty can a few feet along the ditch on Margherita's side. Once he hit it and grunted approval. Better that he should distract himself than have his bored attention suddenly drawn to the gates.

A little more light, a little more colour—browns, grey-

198

greens and yellows; a fiery sliver of pink low in the east. Still no hint of a disturbance within the walls. Salvatore should be clear, Guiseppe biding his time in the chapel enclosure, Carlo ready on the cliff-top, Angelo—

Six twelve . . .

The guard continued with his game for another minute or two then yawned again, rose and dragged the chair into the recess. If something were to catch his eye it would be now; but no. He shuffled along the path, rolling as he went, and blearily Forrester watched him go. He seemed devoid of any capacity for intense alarm or relief; already his night had come to a head, done its worst.

"Can you see Carlo?"

Margherita wriggled to the culvert's rim and looked out and up. "No," she said at last. Her calmness could only be a kind of fatalism.

Six twenty . . . Day was shaping in earnest, pink turning to scarlet, an arc of sun rising above the town. Forrester took a crumpled cigarette from the pack and put it between his teeth, drew out a match. Wait a bit. He checked in his pocket for the car keys, flayed nerves beginning to quicken.

"When I start the fuse, get out your side."

"*D'accordo.* How long now?"

"A few minutes. Keep a watch on the cliff-top. We'll hear the bulldozer first, but keep watching all the same."

Guiseppe over the wall? Carlo would know; he alone could see. Cupping his hands, Forrester lit the cigarette, extinguished the match and flicked it into the ditch. Warm sweat dribbling again; another swift fuse-check. Exactly six-thirty. And silence, a whole minute's silence, stretching mercilessly into a second and a third.

"Holy Mary, Mother of God, pray for—"

Something: a hard metallic thud. Forrester stiffened. Then another, followed by a rattling, dragging sound. He drew on

199

the cigarette; it shook in his lips. Clatter, clatter, and the bulldozer's engine suddenly roared. Make or break for Guiseppe now.

"Tell me when you get the signal—" for the first time in hours Forrester spoke above a whisper. "Shout."

They could hear the bulldozer trundling parallel with the wall, moving farther away from them. The noise seemed to distort as it shuddered into the culvert. It diminished fractionally, as if the engine was idling. The hooks going on? Gear trouble? Guiseppe challenged? . . . All this in the mind. Then, all at once, a guttural snarl and a continuous clanking sound rising together to a crescendo—second after second after second of it until with a tearing, snapping crash something broke and they knew that the bars had ripped away.

Forrester had the short stub of safety-fuse in one hand, the cigarette in the other. A hoarse voice could be heard through the clanking din, urgent, like a bark, and another joined in from near the gates.

"Now!" Margherita called. "*Now!*"

He applied the cigarette; watched the fuse spit alight. Then, like her, he was out, scrambling up the bank as if pursued, head down, running, the confused roar increasing behind them. Seven . . . Eight . . . Nine . . .

First a whipcrack, then a concussive crunch, almost inseparable: the air bounced and discoloured. Across the road Forrester spun in his tracks. Lines of earth spouted where the fuses had been buried and a curdled mass of ochreous smoke bulged and swelled and soared; as if in slow motion he watched one of the gates slowly topple forward and smack down. His head was singing, but he thought he heard a shot.

"Angelo!" Margherita cried, fists raised as if in supplication to the dust. "Angelo!"

And obediently he came, he and Guiseppe, the bulldozer bursting into the open, slewing as it clipped a wall pillar and

200

met the flattened gate, losing direction, missing the culvert and pitching into the ditch, both men leaping clear, up and sprinting.

"Angelo!" Joy in her voice.

Forrester began to move, head turned like someone waiting to receive a relay-baton. A jacketless guard was on the wall, rifle levelled; others were emerging from the thinning dust— three, four.

"Run, Angelo!"

All running now, Angelo and Guiseppe gaining, almost abreast. In rapid succession two shots rang out and Angelo stumbled, fell to his knees. Instinctively, Forrester sprang to him, got a shoulder under his armpit and, with Guiseppe, lifted, ran again, Angelo's legs like a rag-doll's—a small man, slight, fierce-looking, with blood bubbling from his mouth. Scared, Forrester took all this in. Margherita ahead of them, stopped, aghast. Another shot, sobbing off rock. Everything overlapping in a kind of dementia. A hundred yards to the car, some guards in pursuit and Guiseppe suddenly turning, pistol drawn, and firing again and again.

Forrester flung the keys towards Margherita. "Open it!"

Level with the refuse-tip, Angelo growing heavier, dragging, his grey prison-smock spattered red. Guiseppe turned a second time and fired wildly. The pursuit faltered, scattering, going down. Margherita had reached the car and was opening the doors. Angelo coughed, belching blood. Almost there, Margherita coming with arms outstretched and grief such as Forrester had never seen—"Jesus, oh Jesus." Staggering through muck they pitched Angelo into the back seat, Guiseppe and Margherita clambering over him. Forrester flung himself behind the wheel, switched on, slammed into gear. With doors flapping the car crashed out of its covering screen of junk and rusted metal. Over the rough ground, the wheel jarring Forrester's hands, lurching diagonally towards the road, moaning

201

in the back and Guiseppe swearing, winding the window down and leaning out to fire.

Bullets chipped the tarmac in front of them as the car skidded on to the road. Forrester drove like a man possessed, accelerating down the long straight approach to Monteliana.

"Angelo, speak to me ... *Angelo* ..."

39

THROUGH the town, people scattering from the cobbles, everything juddering past in a blur. Through the town and out, throttle and brake and horn, out the other side to where the road curled in a ledge along the hillside. In the mirror Forrester could see they had stripped the smock from Angelo, exposing a gaping exit wound in his chest. Feverishly Guiseppe was ripping his own shirt, Margherita cradling Angelo's head, blood everywhere.

Coming up to the fork. Goats on the road, bounding clear, a scarecrow-like figure waving a stick. And the mind in tatters. Then Salvatore waiting, Carlo too, the car screeching to a standstill, bonnet dipped, dust showering over. And then their faces as they climbed exultantly into the front and discovered what had happened.

For several minutes there was no choice of road. All the voices in the world seemed to be concentrated in the Fiat—a babel of dismay, disbelief, anger, conflict.

"How? ... How?"

"We were halfway—"

"Through the shoulder . . . *Madonna, perde sangue* !"

"We were away. Clear."

"Can he speak?"

"Try and stop that blood. Ayeee—"

"I am, I am."

"*Angelo . . . Angelo, mio.*"

"*Calmo, ragazza, calmo . . .*"

Forrester drove on, foot down. "Where to, for Christ's sake?" No one heard. "Where to?" he shouted.

Alongside, Salvatore stared at him as if he were a stranger. "I'll show you."

"Get off the highway"—Guiseppe, staunching the wound with strips of shirt. "There'll be road-blocks."

"He wants a doctor."

"Keep your advice." White wedges in the corners of Salvatore's veined eyes.

"He'll die otherwise. It's through the lung."

"Drive, and shut up."

The clash of voices never stopped. Still only the one corkscrewing road. Then, suddenly, Salvatore ordered: "Take the track to the left." And Forrester spun the wheel, slowing as he jolted on to an earthen surface that ran between lentil fields. Going north-east. In the mirror Angelo's face was ashen; he'd never live, doctor or no.

For half an hour Forrester drove as Salvatore directed, not once touching a metalled road. Gradually the confusion quietened down: an overall bitterness took its place. They knew about violence, disaster, defeat; bitterness was all they had ever finished with, never the dream.

"Keep his head raised."

"We need water."

"Soon, Margherita."

"Hurry, hurry."

203

"*Calmo* . . ." Salvatore pointed. "That way."

Open scrubland studded with rock. No track, nothing. Hills to the south and wooded country to the north of them. Seven forty-five, only seven forty-five . . . Forrester worked his way across the empty scrub, bearing north-east at Salvatore's urging. By eight they came to a narrow road, turned right and followed it for perhaps a mile until Salvatore said: "Left, now. Into the trees."

A stream glinted through the foliage: Forrester ran the car down to its bank. Reeds and grasses, willows and dappled light. He cut the engine and watched the others lift Angelo and carry him close to the bright water's edge. He stood apart from them and somehow apart from himself, incapable of emotion, and watched them do what they could for Angelo—cupping water to his lips, bathing the wound, wiping his face. The boy lay with his head in Margherita's lap, unaware, it seemed, of their mercies, and only the blood staining the makeshift bandages and occasionally coughing weakly from his mouth pointed to his being alive.

Carlo back and forth to the stream's edge, Guiseppe kneeling shirtless at Angelo's side, Salvatore looking down, still the general—"Moisten his lips if he will not drink . . . Wet more cloth and cool his forehead . . ." Life would crush him yet, crush them all, but they had dignity when it mattered, a natural courage when it mattered, and Forrester knew how separated from them he was.

Even so he touched Salvatore on the elbow. "A doctor might save him," he ventured again. "A doctor, a hospital."

And Salvatore met his gaze as before, as if across a gulf. "Save him for what?" he said.

All the lines in his face were etched deeper. There was a pause, no hatred in it as so often before, no contempt. Salvatore rubbed his eyes with tattooed hands, like someone waking, salt rings showing under his armpits where the sweat had dried. And even before he spoke again Forrester realised he had finally finished with him.

"Go and tell Luigi to come."

"Come where? Here?"

"He will know where."

Angelo coughed again, a gargling sound that made Salvatore swing his head.

"Luigi will want more than my word. You said so yourself."

Salvatore grunted and dug behind his heavy belt into a pocket. He drew out a much-folded square of paper and handed it to Forrester. "You remember everything."

Forrester started to turn away. Then, to his surprise, Salvatore added: "Thank you, friend . . . *Bravo*."

It touched Forrester on the raw. The bandages blackened, but the wounds did not heal, the memories remained. He gazed back at the group by the sparkling water, at Margherita in particular. There were no tears. Only a stoic dignity compounded with the grief and the muttered prayers as she kissed Angelo's dying mask—"Lord have mercy, Christ have mercy, Lord have mercy . . ." Everybody needed help.

40

HE walked through the willows to the car and drove away: his legs weren't too steady. It was unbelievable to be free of duress, but there was still danger. A white Fiat, himself dishevelled, unshaven, blood on his sleeves, blood on the rear seat: if he'd had sense he should have done something about the blood. Eight twenty . . . The hunt would be on, check-points established round the compass. As the crow flies he reckoned he was about halfway between Monteliana and the hut, but exactly where he had no idea. There had been no sign-posts in the fields and scrub. Now he was driving east, the road deserted, his trust in its narrowness; they'd hardly block everything, and perhaps not as far out as this.

He drove as fast as he dared, lifting the dust, exploding birds out of wayside bushes and trees. Farm buildings sometimes standing back from the road, a yoked mule circling a well, a few people tending patches of crops; vaguely he noticed. The hills to the south retreated as he was led more and more to the north-east, but others rose up ahead and before long he was having to use the gears.

He must have covered five or six miles by the time he met a major road: VALLELUNGA 14 kms, S. CATERINA 18 kms. He found the map in the glove-compartment and studied it, then crossed the highway and continued into the hills. Less risk this way; it would bring him round through Alimena to the junction near Enna where Carlo and Guiseppe had mistaken him for someone else and lit the fuse that was to burn towards the flash-point of his own recognition.

"Bravo . . ." No, he thought vehemently, not that; never again was he accepting that. Blindly he'd swallowed it before, lived with the inference of it, risen like a fish to the bait with bombast and bravado yet been spared the hook, the renewed test. From now on nothing could ever be the same again; already he knew this, but he needed time, time to adjust, time to understand.

Below him and far off the land was beginning to haze in the returning heat. Mile by mile the risk of interception receded. Caves high to the left, a wayside shrine to the Virgin, poplars rising like black spires. He pulled into the side and unfolded Salvatore's note. *All well,* he read. *Let them go and hurry over.*

206

Until then—S. It must have been written the evening before, while the dream still held.

Forrester put it away and drove on, thinking increasingly of Inger. But for her he could have escaped overnight—and retained his illusions. So he owed her something; it wasn't all the other way round. From the past in Taormina he remembered the policemen in his room on the morning Nolan had died and one of them asking him: "Why should a man overreach himself?"—and the way his answer had gone: "Perhaps failure to do so would have meant showing her he hadn't sufficient nerve."

Well, there would be no more of that. "Were you a soldier? . . . What is the M.C.? . . ." He would speak to Inger, tell her what he had never told anyone, not knowing it was there to tell. Later, not today or even tomorrow, but not too much later. If such things were important to her she had a right to be told.

He passed Alimena shortly after the half-hour, then made a long, hairpin descent into broken country, crossing a sluggish river with sandy, bush-covered banks. Once in a while a truck or a laden cart shared the road with him, but for the greater part of the way it was his own. He pushed the Fiat hard, his mind surprisingly sharp and lucid, taking stock. The tank was still half full, so there were no immediate worries. But they would hardly get from the hut to Palermo without a refill, and Inger and he hadn't a *lira* between them. He shrugged the thought aside; he could barter his watch, a jacket—something. They'd manage; there were always ways and means. Today was Monday and Palermo offered hotels, banks, remittance facilities . . . The first priority was to reach the hut and complete the formality of their release, fit the correct numberplates, clean out the car, wash, shave, change.

And see her; hold her.

207

In the mirror his face was haggard, blotched with grime. He drove on, recalling with an intensity of feeling Inger's voice, her eyes, her walk, the promise of her smile that could be released at last like a renewal of life. Another part of his mind remained on the look-out for a cruising police car or the dwindling possibility of a check-point, but there was never anything to cause him qualms. Presently a sign-post indicated a place off to the right that he couldn't discover on the map and he ignored it: ahead, and to the north, the land was beginning to take on a familiar desolation. By the clock he had covered about twenty-five kilometres since his dismissal, and again he asked himself where Luigi would make for, what they would do, how it would all end: he could pity them now, each and every one.

He reached the main road ten minutes later and immediately he knew precisely where he was. Almost exactly on nine o'clock he was turning left on to the track that led across the wilderness to the pine-filled hollows in the distance and the hut, stopping only to cover the dried stains on the dark mock-leather seat with one of the blankets still in the boot. As for what was on his sleeves, he could explain that.

41

THE sound of the falls greeted him first: window down, he steered through the pines and the semaphore blink of the sunlight. Well before the hut was in view he started using the horn, and as he nosed the Fiat into the clearing Luigi came clattering down the steps with the shot-gun, calling: "Yes? . . . Yes?"

"Yes." The engine fluttered to a standstill.

"He's out?"—alongside now, thumb hopefully up. "It worked?"

"Out, yes."

Inger appeared in the door and Forrester felt a surge in his heart. Stiffly, he swung his legs and pushed himself from the car, arm lifted in greeting.

"Why the blood?" Suspiciously, Luigi stared. "What happened?"

"I cut myself."

"You?"

As if in partial proof Forrester showed his torn hands. "There was glass in the culvert. Glass and wire."

"What about Angelo?"

"We got him out, I tell you." He moved towards the hut, fumbling for the note, Inger's eyes on him. He could have sworn Luigi was wearing one of his shirts, but he couldn't have cared less. "Here," he said. "Salvatore gave me this."

He left Luigi to read it and quickened his stride, saying: "Inger, Inger—are you all right?"

"I am fine."

He took the steps in one and kissed her clumsily. "Really all right?"

The nervous smile. "Of course."

Then Luigi, good looks screwed against the sun, satisfied, relief emphasising his gestures. "Where did you leave them?"

"By a stream."

"Not at the place?"

"I don't know where that is."

"Why at a stream?"

"They wanted water."

A trace of doubt remaining. "Was anyone hurt? Margherita, Guiseppe—?"

"You've seen what Salvatore says."

"How far from here did you leave them?"

"It's hard to say. I've been cross-country in case of roadblocks, before and since."

"How long ago?"

Forrester's whole body throbbed with fatigue. "Three-quarters of an hour?"

Luigi whistled, but his face brightened. He would know the short cuts; two or three hours were nothing. And all was well . . . He stood in the clearing and looked at them both. "So—it's over. It's good-bye. There's no time to lose."

"*Ciao.*"

"Some girl you've got there."

Forrester tightened his arm round Inger's waist. He grinned wearily, rubbing his beard-stubble.

"Some girl."

Forrester's mind prickled. Luigi started on his way, making for the mildewed boulders and the pines beyond. On the edge of the clearing he turned and called to Inger in that waiter's English of his: "Good-bye, beautiful miss."

Forrester let his arm fall. Uncertainty thickened his voice. "What did he mean?"

Inger shrugged. "That is the way he talks." She separated from him and moved inside the hut. "His English is worse even than mine. All the time it has been the same."

"I'm not asking about his English."

She tossed her hair defensively. "How can I tell what else he said?"

It was more than the phrase; there was the manner of it, the parting look Forrester had intercepted. Oh God, he thought. No . . . No.

"Neal." Now Inger came back. "Neal, you're tired. Was it bad for you? Where are you cut?"

Chequer-board drawn askew on the table, empty glasses, the remains of a candle. Forrester looked past Inger into the room that had been theirs and saw the rumpled blankets on the bed. Even then he doubted, the pain not through to the nerves, incredulity holding jealousy and rage in check. It wasn't to have been like this: it couldn't be.

"Was he in there?"

"Where?"

"There." He jerked his head.

She was silent, motionless. He strode closer and stared in. For seconds on end he stared before something broke and he wheeled on her. "He was, wasn't he? That blatant little bastard was with you."

She didn't flinch from his raw-eyed challenge. "Yes," she said.

"You whore," he stormed. "You bloody whore."

His mind seemed to go beyond rational usefulness. He made for the door, wanting to get out, out, anywhere. He shouldered past Inger into the open and she followed as far as the steps, shouting after him.

"I'm *not*! I'm *not*!"

He didn't listen, yet he heard, and the irony seemed like a final insult.

"I needed somebody. I always need somebody. Neal, *Neal* . . . I'm not like you. I can't manage on my own. I'm afraid on my own."

Forrester found himself by the boulders. He felt sick. A kind of madness pounded inside his skull. Misty spray drifted over him from the skein of falling water, but he was unaware of it, unaware of everything except an enormous bitter hurt that seemed to possess him totally.

211

In dismayed protest his thoughts flitted about for somewhere to settle, something to hold them steady, but in vain. Bitch, they hammered. Bitch—like a futile punctuation-mark scattered through a pattern of images that reached all the way back to the casino at Messina and from there to the Capua and the kidnap on the road and this hut and that room and the raid and his own terror and the hope that had come from it because of her—all this disjointed, feverish, with one clear picture as he saw the parallel between his journey here and that of Luigi's to the rendezvous with the others and what he would find when he arrived.

Bitch.

He lifted his face to the spray, aware of it at last. Gradually the confusion went out of him; his mind hardened, anger in sole charge. He turned from the boulders and crossed the clearing to the hut. Inger was sitting on the steps. She moved her hands when he approached, as if in appeal, but he went on by, avoiding her look. Inside, he rounded the table and went into the barred room, picked up the larger of his suit-cases, flung it on the bed and sprang the catches. There were stubbed cigarettes in saucers on either side of the bed and he kicked at one savagely as he stripped to the waist and sorted fresh clothes.

Number-plates, shave, wash . . . There were practical things to be done.

The feeling of sickness was still there as he walked outside again. "Neal," Inger began as the steps sagged, but he ignored her. The old number-plates had been thrown at the back of the hut amid other rubbish: he retrieved them, returned to the car and extracted the tool-kit. There was refuge of sorts in action. It took him twenty minutes to change the plates and Inger stayed away from him. When he next passed her to get the plastic bucket from the draining-board she was smoking a cigarette, but she made no attempt to speak. Three times he

212

filled the bucket from the falls, twice to shower the car and once to wash the rear seat, using the blanket for that and then to wipe the car roughly over. Then he traced his steps for the final time to the falls and washed himself, standing naked under the bluntness of the water until at last he was clean.

Back in the hut he shaved, after which he dressed, folded the soiled clothes and packed them away, slipped his passport into a hip pocket and turned to leave—coldly, mind made up, the decision taken.

"You too—eh?"—Nolan, at the casino, out of his depth and desperate but afraid to let it show. And Forrester thought with fury: Not quite. Almost, but not quite. At least I didn't finish up dead.

But there were other ways of dying.

He came to the door with his two cases and descended the rickety steps. Only then did Inger rise, touching him, her voice suddenly querulous with alarm.

"What are you doing? Where are you going? . . . *Neal.*"

He shook her off. The sun burned through his shirt. He opened the off-side door and chucked the cases on to the back seat.

"Neal . . . For God's sake!"

Tight-lipped he slid behind the wheel and slammed the door. Inger started beating her knuckles against the window, crying. Without a word or a glance Forrester switched on, dropped into gear and drove away.

213

42

H E turned right when he got to the track. As if he'd
planned in advance he already knew which route he
would take: to Palermo was perhaps seventy miles.
His eyes ached and he reached for his sun-glasses. In and out
of the hollows, then across the stark moon-surface where no
one ever seemed to come.

Afterwards, when he tried to remember this part of the
day, it remained a blank in his mind. He wasn't conscious of
his speed or what else was on the road. He drove as if in a
trance, heedless of the tyre's warning whimper as he cornered
and the centrifugal tug on his body and the rushing pressure
of the warm air; not seeing the plodding woman who raised
a clenched fist in protest as the dust sand-stormed in the Fiat's
wake. Heedless, seething, feeling nothing but the wounds
stabbed into his heart and his pride, knowing only that he'd
been used, mocked, betrayed—and this at the very time when
he could have taken the easy way out.

"*Non toccare*"; Salvatore's words beat around in his brain.
What had she shouted?—"I needed somebody. I always need
somebody . . ." What about me? Is that all I was—somebody?
Just somebody? Another Luigi? . . . Luigi—*that* pigeon-toed
little sod. Forrester spat his disgust through the window.

An arrowed pointer pierced his inattention, jogging the
memory: SULPHUR QUARRIES. But he didn't want re-
minders—of that or of anything. There were some things you
never forgot, never could forget, and this morning was one,
last night another, the entire ghastly week. "You too—eh?" A
time would come when he could reason, but it wasn't now.
Bitch. The self-centred spin of his mind only stopped once.

God, he should have known. If that's the way you are, he thought, couldn't you have waited? At least couldn't you have done that?

The road was going berserk, trying to find a way through a savage range of hills: more and more it forced him to concentrate. He sounded the horn on a succession of blind bends, negotiating each of which was like an act of faith, came out of them and climbed through the gears only to be met by others, made to brake, change down again, swing the wheel as if he were on a roller-coaster. The NO OVERTAKING signs were farcical. Ten to eleven, the tank still a quarter full . . .

She'll manage. She'll thumb a lift when she reaches the highway. The world was full of men.

Further wayside information—PALERMO, 85 kms . . . Another snaking stretch. And Forrester's mind and heart still burning, still vicious. Then, as the car topped a slight rise, he saw something that shrivelled his mood into a hard knot of dread, bringing him sharply to his senses.

A double row of tar barrels blocked the road, an army truck behind them, soldiers, an officer astride the crown of the camber, reaching for his pistol as Forrester slammed on the brakes and the car screamed to a standstill.

Two of the soldiers ran forward belligerently. "Out," the officer ordered curtly in the sudden silence. He jerked the pistol sideways as if he were tapping something. "Out."

Forrester obeyed without hesitation. One of the men was already at the boot, the other opening a rear door, poking about inside. The officer came closer, studying the number-plates; he was young and whippet-thin, with quick darting eyes. Forrester's fear was entirely cerebral: it wasn't a physical thing; yet this was how it always began. At last he could measure himself, even as he stood there, scared. There would be no running from this.

215

"Yes?" he said shakily.

"Your car?"

"No, rented."

Until then the officer must have assumed Forrester was a compatriot. But the white 1800 Fiat weighed with him more.

"Where are you from?"

Forrester jerked a thumb over his shoulder. "Back there."

"Where?"

"Taormina way."

"And you are going—?"

"To Palermo."

"Your name?" The questions were coming rapid-fire.

"Forrester."

"Nationality?"

"British."

"Your passport, *per favore*."

Forrester drew it from his pocket. The "please" was a hopeful indication, but if they decided to search the luggage his chances would be stone dead.

The officer holstered his pistol, then turned the passport's pages with deliberation. His cap's black leather chin-strap hung loosely round his pointed jaw. He didn't look like a Sicilian.

"There is a police stamp here." Echoes of Salvatore. He twisted the passport upside-down. "Taormina."

"A man committed suicide in my hotel. I was asked to go to the police-post to make a statement."

"You knew him?"

"No. But he was in the room next to mine."

A frown. "This was six days ago."

"That's right." Sidelong he could see the soldier had dumped the two cases on the road and was probing under the seat, which he'd lifted. With an effort Forrester fought down the urge to bluster.

216

"And today your route has been——?"

"Through Leonforte."

"Thank you, *signore*." The passport was handed back, but the luggage was still in the road. "Have you seen another white Fiat, by any chance?"

"Today?"

"Yes."

"Not that I can remember."

One of the soldiers reported: "Nothing in the car, *tenente*. What about the cases?"

"Put them back in," the officer said, and a spasm of relief visibly plucked Forrester's mouth.

He tried to smile politely; an innocent visitor. "Is that all?"

"*Sì, grazie.*"

"What's this all about, anyway?"

"There has been some trouble to the south. Wild men, bandits. They blew the gates off the lock-up at Monteliana and a prisoner escaped. They were using a car like this—hence our thoroughness, *signore*, for which you must forgive me."

"*Prego.*" Forrester sat in the car and pulled the door to. "D'you think you'll get them?"

"For certain," the officer said. "Not here, maybe, but somewhere. It is only a question of time. One of the men was wounded. Wild men, *signore*, trash; people with more courage than sense." He drew himself up and saluted casually. "*Va bene*. A pleasant journey." Then, to the soldiers: "All right. Move the barrels."

43

FORRESTER had covered half a mile or so before the giddiness and the reaction came. He pulled abruptly into the side and switched off, crossed his arms on the wheel and let his head sink down.

Acceptance was the first essential, acceptance of what he was. There was no other base on which to build and make sense of himself or what had happened. Instinctively he understood, head on arms and silence all around, the scene by the water's edge beneath the willows swimming in the darkness of his mind. "We are not what we are from choice . . ." Maybe. But they knew what they were; there were no veneers, no doubts about the make-up of their natures or the limits to which they could go without breaking. And in their grief and bitterness there was acceptance of the cost. It had always been so, and would be again, even when they were run to earth: four days with them had taught him that. Famished, hunted, dying, alive and pathetic—they would take it as they would have taken triumph and the fulfilment of the dream, because this was life, all part of life, and they fought life with themselves and not with some version which they were not.

He had done that. Forrester raised his head. Time and again, the latent flaw in him unrecognised, smothered by events. Even when Inger had said: "Don't expect too much . . . Trouble comes of expecting too much," he hadn't understood. Behind the façade he presented to the world a tiny fretful part of him distorted his judgment, turning its need, its frailty under pressure, into the belief and vanity that he too was indispensable.

He listened to his thoughts. *He* was the odd man out. Inger

218

had no delusions about herself, either. "I'm afraid on my own. I'm not like you . . ." The words stung. He had survived so much, fooled himself, fooled others. And it had to stop: as of now there had to be a new beginning. You could die a death of sorts yet start again, honestly, face to face with yourself, recognising what you saw. And perhaps one day you could look back and reflect without pain on the redemptive opportunities of time and chance.

His bruised mind couldn't grapple with it all. For a long time he stared at the road and the dun-coloured hills to either side. He didn't like what he was, and he'd never been what he liked. One abandoned moment of terror, one hissed *"Don't move!"* and the paralysis that followed—these were enough to open his eyes. But there was no going back. He could grow now; mature at last.

With pity he thought of the group of them by the stream: at least he had retained pity. They'd never know, but he owed them something—even Luigi, still making for the rendezvous perhaps, still with his own disillusionment to come. And Inger? . . . She would survive. She knew what she was and she took what she could, like a child.

"You too—eh?"

No, he thought yet again. No, thank God.

But he couldn't leave her there. It was no way to begin. Or could he? . . . For a good minute the decision balanced in his mind before he turned the car and started back the way he had come.

The officer at the check-point seemed to think he had returned to report a sighting.

"What is it, then?"

"I left my camera in Leonforte. In a bar, there."

A sympathetic cluck of the tongue. They rolled the barrels away to let the car nose through. *"Arrivederci,"* the officer said, as if to imply that they would be meeting again. But already Forrester had decided against that. There were other roads: when he found her, if he found her, he would head north and make for the coast— Cefalú, Términi . . .

Thirty minutes after acknowledging the officer's parting wave Forrester reached the track. And there, a good quarter of a mile along it, he saw Inger. The blue trouser-suit stood out against the bare, bleached, desolate expanses: she was lugging her two cases, and even at that range he could tell that she limped.

And he felt nothing. Nothing—either way.

He ran the car towards her until he found a suitable place to make a three-point turn. Then he waited, watching in the mirror as she covered the last fifty yards or so, leaning over to open the off-side door as she approached. Without so much as a glance at him she limped level, pushed the cases ahead of her and got in. Not a word between them. Her face was stern, beaded with sweat as she slid off her shoes and leaned back, closing her eyes.

Forrester bumped slowly across the rough ground until they reached the road, then swung left. Nicosia, Cefalú, Términi . . .

"As far as your Consul," he said.

For regular early information

about

FORTHCOMING NOVELS

send a postcard

giving your name and address

to

MRS JEAN POVEY

HODDER & STOUGHTON LTD.

St. Paul's House,
Warwick Lane,
London, E.C.4.